EARTH

IN

TROUBLE

N.S.S. RAMAKRISHNA

EARTH IN TROUBLE

Author:
N.S.S. Ramakrishna
H.No. 8-8/6/6, Plot No. 223/2, Road No.7,
Hemanagar, Hyderabad-500039
Email: nssramakrishna.dop@gmail.com
Mobile: 9573045062, 9440195062

Editor: Smt. Sahaja Sayini

First Published by Notion Press 2024
Copyright @ N.S.S.Ramakrishna
@RoC No. L-152582/2024 dt. 14-08-2024
issued by Registrar of Copyrights, Govt.of
India, New Delhi.

Dedication

To my parents who created me

*(Sri Neelamraju Mohan Rao
&
Smt. Sri Durga Rajyalakshmi)*

Preface and Acknowledgements

For a long time, I had numerous thoughts lingering in my mind, hidden away in my old diaries for years. I never dared to put my ideas on paper for publication.

I used to write poetry, articles, and stories, many of which were published in various newspapers and magazines.

In 2002, my Hindi literary work "भारत में नागर विमानन" (Civil Aviation in India) received appreciation from the Ministry of Civil Aviation.

After that, I did not attempt any further literary work.

However, witnessing the current state of the world, I felt motivated to write a novelette.

From childhood, I have read epics, spiritual books from various religions, and works on culture, astrology, astronomy, science, and philosophy. I have always tried to connect all these theories to draw conclusions, which sometimes makes me appear deeply religious and, at other times, like an atheist.

The present story, Earth in Trouble, includes elements of love, sentiment, suspense, mystery, investigation, war, and social and corporate responsibility. The story begins on a college campus and leads into space. I do not wish to reveal more about the content, and I encourage readers to discover it for themselves.

I would like to specially mention **Smt. Sahaja Sayini** for helping me shape this book, and my sincere thanks to her for making it possible.

On a personal note, I would also like to thank my wife **Phani Kumari**, my daughter **Shri Divya**, and my son **Karthik**, for their patience and support during this process.

As per the Rule. 8 (3) of CCS (Conduct) Rules, 1964 of Gov. of India, being a Government Servant, I hereby declare that the views expressed by me are of my own and not that of Government.

*****

1

Excuse me," a gentle voice chimed from behind, like a melody drifting on a summer breeze, accompanied by the softest of taps upon George's shoulder. With a graceful pivot, he turned away from the lively cadence of his conversation with friends, drawn by the allure of the unexpected interruption.

"Hi, I'm Sam," the new comer introduced himself with warmth that mirrored the soft glow of dawn breaking over the horizon, his smile a beacon of hospitality. "Could you lend me a hand in locating Block C?" he inquired, his eyes alight with a blend of curiosity and determination. "Blocks A and B stand before us, but C seems to have eluded my gaze."

"Yeah, of course," George responded with a reassuring nod, his willingness to assist echoing the gentle sway of a willow in a calming breeze. "I'm actually headed in that direction towards my hostel room, it's nearby. Join me," he offered warmly, extending an invitation with the ease of a seasoned host. "Oh, and I'm George, by the way," he added, his name slipping effortlessly from his lips like a familiar melody.

As they set off towards the hostel, their conversation flowed seamlessly, weaving through topics like a river meandering through lush meadows. Each step they took seemed to sync with the lively rhythm of the bustling morning around them. The sun, peeking through the clouds, cast a gentle glow upon the streets, painting the scene with hues of warmth and possibility. Despite the hint of a light drizzle, the air carried a refreshing coolness, a welcome respite from the impending monsoon season in Hyderabad, India. It was as if nature itself was orchestrating a symphony of sensations, inviting them to embrace the beauty of the moment.

Hyderabad, a city steeped in both historical grandeur and modern innovation, beckons travelers with its myriad charms.

Renowned as a vibrant hub of tourism, it also proudly wears the mantle of a prominent software destination. Global corporations dotting its western landscape attest to its status as a bustling technological epicenter, where innovation thrives amidst tradition.

Often likened to a microcosm of India itself, Hyderabad embraces diversity with open arms, offering a sanctuary where people from all corners of the globe can find solace and belonging. Its rich tapestry of culture, cuisine, and customs reflects the mosaic of the nation it represents.

With a storied past spanning over four centuries, Hyderabad stands as a testament to resilience and evolution. From the majestic architecture of its historic monuments to the gleaming skyscrapers of its modern skyline, each edifice whispers tales of bygone eras and contemporary triumphs.

In essence, Hyderabad is more than just a city; it's a living, breathing testament to the beauty of diversity, the resilience of heritage, and the boundless spirit of innovation.

The inception of the Bharath School of Business (BSB) marked a pivotal moment in the landscape of Asian education. Conceived to fulfil the growing demand for a world-class business school in the region, BSB emerged from the collective vision of luminaries from both corporate and academic spheres.

As the gates of BSB opened to welcomea new wave of eager students, the gentle drizzle that enveloped the campus seemed to mirror the institution's embrace. Like a nurturing gesture from nature itself, the rain whispered promises of growth, renewal, and opportunity to those who crossed its threshold.

Amidst the backdrop of rain-kissed greenery and the hum of anticipation, BSB stood as a beacon of excellence, poised to mould the future leaders of tomorrow.

With each passing year, BSB's campus undergoes a subtle transformation, akin to the turning of seasons. It evolves and rejuvenates itself, mirroring the journey of its students as they embark on their educational odyssey. With every new batch that graces its halls, the campus breathes anew, infused with the vibrancy and enthusiasm of those who come to seek knowledge and inspiration within its hallowed walls.

Each arriving student bore not only their belongings but also their hopes and dreams, their footsteps echoing the cadenceof aspirations set in motion.

Symbolic directional boards, akin to compass needles pointing toward uncharted territories, stood as silent sentinels guiding these eager souls towards their future destinations.

Amidst the bustling throng, senior students moved with the assured grace of seasoned navigators, their familiarity with the terrain akin to that of lions surveying their domain. Confident and purposeful, they roamed the campus with an air of authority, embodying the spirit of leadership and mentorship.

In contrast, the new arrivals, their hearts aflutter with excitement and apprehension, resembled deer cautiously venturing into uncharted realms. Navigating the labyrinthine paths of academia, they tread with cautious steps, their eyes wide with wonder at the vast expanse of possibilities unfolding before them.

In this dynamic ecosystem of learning and discovery, the BSB campus pulsed with the juxtaposition of confidence and uncertainty, anticipation and trepidation, each element converging to shape the narrative of a new academic year.

Close by, the cafeteria bustled with the harmonious symphony of laughter and conversation, its walls reverberating with the joyful camaraderie of newfound companionship. Groups of students, like tightly-knit teams, gathered around tables adorned with trays of culinary delights, their spirits lifted by the warmth of shared experiences and the promise of budding friendships.

Amidst the lively chatter and clinking

of cutlery, bonds forged in the crucible of shared learning and discovery grew stronger with each passing moment. Laughter echoed like a melody, weaving through the air like a thread stitching hearts together, as students exchanged tales of triumphs and tribulations, aspirations and ambitions.

In this bustling hub of social interaction, the cafeteria served not only as a refueling station for the body but also as a sanctuary for the soul—a place where connections were forged, memories were made, and the tapestry of student life was woven with threads of camaraderie and companionship.

With a casual air, George inquired, "By the way, what's your room number?"

Sam, still grappling with the labyrinthine layout of the hostel, hesitated before replying, "It's, um, C143."

A playful glint danced in George's eyes as he remarked, "Oh, really? Interesting number. Do you happen to know the meaning of the code 143?"

Puzzled, Sam shook his head. "No, what does it mean?"

Pausing in front of a door, George flashed a mischievous smile. "Here is your room!"

Grateful, Sam extended his hand, expressing his thanks. "Thank you, George. That is very kind of you. But seriously, what does 143 mean?"

With a chuckle, George revealed the meaning, "'I love you'."

Their laughter echoed through the corridor as they shared in the light-hearted moment, two new found friends embracing the serendipitous joy of connection.

As George lent a hand in unpacking, he posed the question, "Where are you from?"

"I'm from Siliguri, in West Bengal. Currently, I'm serving as the CFO of SONAI in Al Jubail," Sam replied, his voice tinged with the echoes of distant places and professional endeavors. "And you?"

"I hail from Kerala, a South Indian state often referred to as God's Own Country," George responded with a hint of pride in his heritage.

Curiosity piqued, George continued their exchange, asking, "What course are you taking?"

"In the Fifteen Months PGPMAX program," Sam revealed. "And what about you?"

George reciprocated the inquiry, fostering a conversation that wove together the threads of their backgrounds, aspirations, and academic pursuits.

"I'm doing a one-year Master's," George mentioned before excusing himself momentarily to take a call.

While George attended to his phone conversation outside, Sam took the opportunity to complete the remaining formalities before settling onto the bed, his gaze drifting thoughtfully out the window.

Upon George's return, he declared, "Okay, Sam, looks like you're all set. Let's head to the cafeteria. I'll introduce you to my friends."

With a nod of agreement, Sam grabbed his phone, and together they made their way to the bustling heart of campus life. George's friends greeted them warmly as they entered,and George wasted no time in extolling the virtues of their surroundings.

"This place has amazing energy, and the coffee here is incredible. You have to try it," George insisted with a smile, his enthusiasm infectious.

Grateful for the warm welcome and eager to immerse himself in the vibrant atmosphere, Sam nodded in appreciation, feeling a sense of belonging beginning to takeroot within him.

As they approached George's friends, he wasted no time in making introductions, his smile radiating warmth and camaraderie. "Hi, guys! Meet Sam, a seasoned professional from SONAI," George announced proudly.

With grace, Sam extended his hand, his demeanor poised and affable. "Nice to meet you all," he greeted warmly as he shook handswith each of them in turn.

In response, Zain, Alex, Riya, and Ravi reciprocated with genuine smiles and friendly gestures, their welcoming demeanor fostering an atmosphere of camaraderie and inclusion. With each exchange, bonds began to form, weaving a tapestry of friendship and connection that promised to enrich the daysahead.

"Wait, where is she? This woman is always busy doing something," George huffed, playfully scanning the bustling cafeteria.

Just then, a familiar voice cut through the chatter, accompanied by the sound of approaching footsteps. "Hi George, Hi everyone!" greeted Lisa with a bright smile as she entered the scene.

George couldn't resist a teasing remark."Hi Lisa, where have you been?"

he interrogated, his tone light hearted yet filledwith mock seriousness.

Breathless from her hurried arrival, Lisa offered her explanation. "Sorry, guys, I was in the library looking for something," she explained, her words punctuated by a slight gasp for air.

Her tardiness elicited a chuckle from Zain. "As expected," he remarked his tone affectionate yet teasing. The group joined in, laughter bubbling forth at the familiar scene, their bond strengthened by the shared moments of camaraderie and jest.

"Anyway, Lisa, this is..." George began, intending to introduce Sam to Lisa.

But before he could finish, Lisa's face lit up with recognition, and she interjected enthusiastically, "Hi, Sam! Oh my god! After a long time. How have you been?"

Surprised by the sudden familiarity, George interrupted with astonishment, "Youguys know each other?"

With a smile, Lisa began to explain,

"Remember I told you I attended a conference in the US last year? We met there."

Sam nodded in confirmation, his own smile mirroring Lisa's excitement. "Yes, we met there. It's been a long time technically, but that conference seems like yesterday to me. Thanks for asking. I'm fine, Lisa. How are you? How's your life been?" he replied warmly, the years between their meetings melting away in the warmth of their rekindled connection.

"It's been great since then. I think I already told you this, Sam, but the presentation you gave on Yoga was wonderful. It really inspired me to learn more about it, and thanks to you, now I've incorporated the habit of doing it every single day. It's one of the factors that brought me to India to pursue my higher studies," Lisa shared, her smile radiating genuine gratitude and enthusiasm.

Sam listened attentively, touched by the impact his presentation had made on Lisa's life. "I'm glad to hear that, Lisa. It's amazing how something as simple as

Yoga can have such a profound effect. I'm honored to have played a part in your journey," he replied warmly, his own smile reflecting the joy of knowing he had made a difference.

Their conversation continued, weaving through reminiscences of the conference and the shared passion for Yoga, cementing their bond over shared interests and experiences. In this moment of connection and camaraderie, the distance between past and present melted away, leaving only the warmth of friendship and shared memories to light their path forward.

"In this vast world, isn't it remarkable how our paths intertwine? Lisa and I share a history, while Zain and Riya welcomed me on my very first day. Through them, I met Alex and Ravi, and now, it seems George will become my guide in the days ahead. And yet, here we all are, gathered in this cozy cafeteria. It's truly a marvel, isn't it?" remarked Sam, his voice filled with wonder at the serendipitous connections they shared.

"That's right," everyone murmured in

agreement, their eyes reflecting the sharedsentiment.

"We may never know whether it's mere coincidence or the hand of destiny," Sam concluded with a thoughtful smile, leaving the question to linger in the air as they continued to savor the moment together.

In that intimate space, amidst the laughter and camaraderie, they found solace in the beauty of their interconnected lives, each thread weaving seamlessly into the tapestry of their shared experiences. And as they basked in the warmth of friendship and serendipity, they couldn't help but marvel at the mysterious ways in which life brought them together.

* * * * *

2

"Corporate Social Responsibility," Professor Shah elucidated, his voice commanding attention as it resonated through the lecture hall, seamlessly navigating the slides of his PowerPoint Presentation. "It is a form of international private business self- regulation," he began, his tone authoritative yet inviting, drawing the students into the discourse. "It aims to contribute to societal goals of a philanthropic, activist, or charitable nature by engaging in or supporting volunteering or ethically-oriented practices."

As the students leaned forward, their focus unwavering, Shah continued to unravel the complexities of CSR with precision and clarity. "In the recent past," he elaborated, "it has moved considerably from voluntary decisions at the level of individual organizations to mandatory schemes at regional, national, and international levels." His words underscored the dynamic evolution of CSR, underscoring its growing significance in shaping the ethical landscape of global business practices.

In that lecture hall, amidst the hum of engagement and the flicker of projector light, Professor Shah painted a vivid portrait of CSR as not just a corporate obligation, but a moral imperative driving positive change in societies worldwide.

As the slides transitioned seamlessly under Professor Shah's guidance, each new image and piece of information shed light on different facets of Corporate Social Responsibility (CSR), deepening the understanding of his attentive audience.

Then, amidst the atmosphere of intellectual curiosity, a question emerged: "When did this concept of Corporate evolve?"

Pausing momentarily to consider the query, Professor Shah gracefully addressed the historical origins of CSR, tracing its evolution through the annals of business history. With eloquence and insight, he delved into the roots of CSR, highlighting key milestones and pivotal moments that shaped its emergence as a fundamental aspect of modern corporate governance.

In his response, Professor Shah not only imparted knowledge but also ignited a spark of inquiry, inspiring his students to explore further the intricate tapestry of CSR and its profound impact on the world of business and beyond.

The tale traced its origins back to the tumultuous era of the Industrial Revolution, a transformative period that swept through Europe, particularly in Britain and the United States, spanning roughly from 1760 to 1840. This epochal shift marked the transition from age-old hand production methods to the mechanized marvels of the machine age.

As the landscape of industry underwent a seismic transformation, new chemical and iron production processes emerged, fueled by the inexorable march of progress. Steam and water power surged to the forefront, propelling innovation forward, while the development of machine tools revolutionized manufacturing processes. Against this backdrop, the mechanized factory system rose to prominence, heralding a new dawn of mass production and industrialization.

Concurrently, amidst the clatter of machinery and the ceaseless hum of progress, the Industrial Revolution bore witness to an unprecedented surge in population growth. The confluence of these factors created a fertile ground for the inception of Corporate Social Responsibility, as societal challenges and ethical imperatives began to intersect with the burgeoning forces of commerce and industry.

"In an era where the ethos of the business realm significantly shapes societal values and determines the prospects of future generations, it becomes imperative to scrutinize and broaden the objectives and aspirations of commerce," Samson asserted, his voice resonating with conviction and purpose.

"Indeed," the Professor concurred,

nodding in agreement, acknowledging the validity of the argument. In that moment of shared understanding, the importance of critically examining the role of business in society became palpable, setting the stage for deeper exploration and meaningful dialogue on the principles of Corporate Social Responsibility and their profound impact on the world at large.

"Egocentric ethics perpetuates the notion that humans are inherently competitive beings, and that capitalism is the innate economic system," Samson elucidated, his words cutting through the air with precision. "This perspective leads to the belief that ecological consequences are extraneous to human economic activities and thus should not be subject to scrutiny. In reality, it exacerbates the growing divide between the affluent and the impoverished."

"In contrast," he continued, his voice unwavering, "homocentric ethics transcends individual self-interest to prioritize the collective welfare. However, it operates under the assumption of human superiority, justifying the exploitation of the naturalworld for human gain."

With each assertion, Samson peeled back the layers of ethical discourse, exposing the complexities inherent in human interactions with the environment and each other. His words sparked contemplation, inviting his audience to critically examine prevailing ideologies and their implications for the future of humanity and the planet.

"The eco-centric ethical approach," the Professor expounded, his voice carrying theweight of conviction, "offers a pathway to harmonizing human advancement with the preservation of our natural environment."

He continued to elaborate, his words painting a vivid picture of sustainable practices and conscientious stewardship. "This approach encompasses various sustainable practices, including the enhancement of eco-efficiency, which not only benefits the bottom line but also minimizes environmental impact. Moreover, it entails the innovation of products and services that adhere to stringent environmental standards, as well as the development of production processes that prioritize resource conservation and circularity."

"Furthermore," he continued, his tone unwavering, "ecocentric ethics advocates for industry-wide self-regulation and proactive engagement with legislation to foster environmental stewardship."

With a pause, the Professor concluded, his words imbued with a sense of urgency and hope, "These sustainable practices represent tangible steps towards achieving a symbiotic relationship between human prosperity and the preservation of our precious natural world."

"What is destroying the earth?" a student's voice pierced the silence, echoing the collective concern of the room. "We are simultaneously disrupting the system and attempting to mitigate the damage separately. Can't we work together?"

"A valid point," the Professor acknowledged with a solemn nod before delving into the heart of the matter.

"With oil spills, a deluge of plastic waste, and toxic chemicals infiltrating our waterways, we are jeopardizing the most precious resource our planet possesses," he began, his voice tinged with urgency. "Environmental degradation occurs as a result of the depletion of Earth's natural resources and the compromising of its delicate ecosystems. This manifests in various forms, from the extinction of species to pollution in the air, water, and soil. Coupled with the exponential growth of human population, environmental degradation emerges as one of the foremost threats facing our world today."

As his words hung in the air, the weight of their implications settled upon the listeners, urging them to contemplate the gravity of their collective responsibility. At that point of shared awareness, the call for unity and concerted action reverberated through the room, igniting a spark of determination to confront the challenges ahead with resolve and solidarity.

"Sir, if wild mammals were to question our treatment of them, applying the same principle to us, what could be our answer?" Sam's inquiry hung in the air, a poignant reflection of humanity's impact on the naturalworld.

The Professor's expression turned grave as he contemplated the stark reality presented by Sam's question. "Humans, despite comprising just 0.01% of all life on Earth, have been responsible for the destruction of 83% of wild mammals," he stated, his voice heavy with regret. "If extraterrestrials of a more advanced race were to judge us by the same standards, viewing us as we view wild mammals, what defense could we possibly offer? There is no justification for our actions."

A solemn silence descended upon the room as the weight of the Professor's words settled upon the gathered students, prompting them to confront the uncomfortable truth of humanity's impact on the world around them. At that point of collective reckoning, the urgent need for change echoed through the room, urging them to heed the call of responsibility and take meaningful action to safeguard the future of all life on Earth.

"If it happens, what will happen?" George's question hung in the air, laden with apprehension.

The Professor's response was sombre, his sigh a lament for the state of humanity. With a pause that stretched into eternity, a sad, resigned smile graced his lips as he uttered, "All will perish, leaving the space to them."

At that juncture, the weight of his words settled heavily upon the room, a stark reminder of the fragility of human existence and the profound impact of our actions on the world around us. The sombre realization that we are but fleeting inhabitants of a planet teeming with life served as a sobering call to reflection and responsibility, urging each individual to consider their role in shaping the fate of humanity and the natural world.

Samson, his voice tinged with emotion, interjected with a solemn pronouncement. "However, political will and Corporate Social Responsibility can be our saving grace." His gaze turned inward, his thoughts haunted by the rapid degradation wrought by humanity's unchecked pursuit of progress.

"Sir," he continued, his tone heavy withsorrow, "since the emergence of the Industrial Revolution in the modern era, thesituation has spiraled from bad to worse in just 200 years. Our planet has sustained its ecological balance for billions of years, yet our relentless pursuit of development, science, corporations, and globalization has brought us to the brink of catastrophe. We'vetraded comfort for the future of our planet, and the cost may be more than we can bear."

In those solemn words, Samson articulated a profound truth about the perilous state of our world and the urgent need for collective action. His impassioned plea for political will and Corporate Social

Responsibility served as a beacon of hope in the face of adversity, reminding his audience that it is never too late to change course and strive for a more sustainable and equitable future for all.

"Well said, Sam," the Professor commended, acknowledging the gravity of his words. "But perhaps, during our evolution, such upheaval is unavoidable. However, there may come a day when we achieve a state of peace and prosperity without adverse effects."

Samson's response was swift and impassioned. "Through experience? We need not endure every trial to foresee the outcome. Our trajectory must shift entirely. Development, as it stands, serves only to enhance comfort, neglecting the true wellbeing of humanity."

With a nod, the Professor concluded, his gaze resting upon the assembled students. "Hope lies in the hands of the coming generations, led by youngsters like you. Perhaps you will be the ones to change the rules of the game."

As the discussion drew to a close, the Professor beckoned Sam to his chambers, a silent invitation for further discourse and contemplation.

* * * * *

"Hey Sam, why the aggression today?" Lisa inquired, her smile attempting to diffuse the tension in the room.

Sam's response was impassioned, his frustration evident in his words. "The initiatives to save this planet are disproportionate to the destructive activities occurring. We're hurtling towards disaster at a speed of 100 kilometers per hour, while our efforts to counteract it move at a mere 1 kilometer per hour. If this pace continues, there will be no future for the coming generations."

His words hung heavy in the air, a stark reminder of the urgency of the situation and the imperative for immediate action. In that moment of raw honesty, the gravity of the environmental crisis weighed heavily on their hearts, propelling them to confront the uncomfortable truth and redouble their efforts to effect meaningful change.

Lisa nodded in agreement. "True. But sometimes, we must accept that we can't fix everything and simply go with the flow," sheremarked, her tone resigned.

But Sam's resolve remained unshaken. "No. Wherever we are, we should strive to change the rules of the game at our level. That should be our motto, and I'm determined to play my part," he asserted, his hope shining through despite the bleakness of the situation.

"That's good," Lisa said, her eyes brightening with a spark of hope. "If like-minded people like us can reach positions where we can make decisions for humanity, then we can contribute to some positive change."

George, a silent spectator throughout the discussion, quietly absorbed the exchange, his contemplative expression hinting at the thoughts brewing in his mind. At that instant of shared conviction and determination, the seeds of change were sown, inspiring each individual to embrace their role as agents of progress and transformation in the face of adversity.

* * * * *

"Good morning, Sir," Sam greeted Professor Shah as he entered the room.

"Very good morning, my son. Come, come," the Professor warmly invited him in. "Let us have a cup of tea."

"No thanks, Sir," Sam replied, taking aseat beside him.

"Sam," the Professor began, his tone filled with admiration, "I have completed 30 years of service in the teaching field, and I have never come across a student like you. Your aspirations, thoughts, ideals, and vision are truly remarkable. I wish for you to reach new heights where you can fulfil your dreams and achieve your aspirations."

With heartfelt sincerity, the Professor handed Sam a large packet of books. "These are for you," he said. "All the best in your journey."

Sam accepted the books with gratitude, feeling the weight of the Professor's faith and blessings. In that instance, the bond between mentor and student transcended the confines of academia, embodying the timeless spirit of guidance, encouragement, and belief in the potential of the human spirit to soar to greater heights.

* * * * *

3

"Let's go!" Sam smiled as he spoke.

They started walking toward the main gate, the warm sun casting long shadows on the pathway. Suddenly, Riya's voice rang out from behind. "Lisa! Lisa!"

Lisa turned around to see Riya running up, slightly out of breath and waving a hand to get her attention. "Professor Amit was asking about some reference document," Riya gasped, trying to catch her breath.

"Oh, shit! I forgot. Thanks, Riya!" Lisa exclaimed, a look of realization crossing her face. She mentally kicked herself for the oversight.

"Have some water," George offered, holding out a water bottle with a concerned expression.

"No, George. I'm fine. Thanks for offering," Riya smiled, politely declining the bottle. She appreciated his thoughtfulness, even in such a small gesture.

"Guys, please give me a minute. I have a small task with Professor Amit. I'll be back in a minute," Lisa said, already preparing to head back. She adjusted her bag on her shoulder and turned back toward the academic building with a sense of urgency.

"How many hours is a minute?" George teased, raising an eyebrow.

Lisa gave George a serious look, her lips pressed into a thin line before turning to follow Riya and rushing back into the block. George watched her retreat with an exaggerated sigh, shaking his head with a smirk.

After a while, as they waited under the shade of the large tree, George grew increasingly impatient. He tapped his foot and glanced at Sam, who was lying down on the grass, looking entirely at ease. George couldn't hold back his frustration any longer. "Ugh! How long will this woman take to come back? She just has to submit the document. I'm sure she must be discussing something else and forgot about us."

Sam, maintaining his calm demeanor, signaled George to come and lie down next to him. "Relax, George. Take a break," he suggested, patting the spot beside him.

George exhaled sharply but obliged, lying down next to Sam. As he settled down, he felt the tension in his body begin to ease. The cool breeze rustling through the leaves above and the soft chatter of students in the distance created a soothing atmosphere.

"I don't understand you, Sam," George said, his frustration melting into curiosity. "How are you this patient all the time? You seem like some utopian citizen to me. You always appear to be missing something. I've never met a person like you before. What's your secret?"

"Secret... for what?" Sam questioned with a smile, tilting his head slightly.

George paused for a moment, rubbing his chin thoughtfully before breaking into a grin. "Yeah! I got it now. It's either becauseyou don't have a girlfriend or you're definitely not from this planet."

Sam chuckled, his eyes twinkling with amusement. "Do you want to know my secret? I have patience because I have a friend called George." He laughed, the sound light and genuine.

"Yeah, right! I am incredible," George replied sarcastically, rolling his eyes. But then he sobered, looking at Sam with genuine appreciation. "But on a serious note, Sam, you're an amazing person."

Gazing at the stars, Sam's expression turned contemplative. The sky above was a canvas of twinkling lights, each star a reminder of the vastness of the universe. He turned to George and said seriously, "I'm scared that you're going to kiss me now."

Both burst out laughing, the sound of their laughter carrying through the quiet night. The tension from earlier dissolved completely, replaced by a profound sense of camaraderie. They lay back on the grass, shoulders touching, and continued to gaze up at the star-studded sky.

After a few minutes of silence, George looked up at the dark sky, the stars twinkling like distant beacons of hope. "You know, Sam, sometimes I get so scared when I look at the sky. You wanna know why?" He paused, gathering his thoughts, his voice tinged with vulnerability. "Every day we wake up to the sun, work, work, and work for something—for establishing our names, for relationships. But at night, when I look at the sky, I feel like I am all alone, just a human being living on this planet Earth like everyone else."

He sighed deeply, the exhalation carrying the weight of his introspection into the cool night air. "I feel a sense of inferiority complex. I feel like we know so little about everything. The vastness of the universe makes all our struggles, all our ambitions, seem so insignificant. I feel... unimportant."

George's eyes remained fixed on the sky, the stars reflecting in his gaze as if he were searching for answers among them. "It's like, during the day, we're these busy little ants, always working towards something, always moving. But at night, when the sky stretches out endlessly above us, it's a reminder of how small we really are. How fleeting our lives are in the grand scheme of things."

He turned to look at Sam, his expression a mix of frustration and wonder. "Doesn't it ever get to you? The thought that no matter how hard we try, we're just tiny specks in this immense universe? That our knowledge is just a drop in the ocean compared to what's out there?"

Sam, still gazing at the stars, replied, "I know exactly what you're talking about, George. You know what I feel? Everyone is important. We are chosen by nature. Our existence has a purpose. A living being evolves from a stage of having no will to a stage where it can use it's will to alter its environment. Each one of us carries the responsibility of balancing and protecting the universe, even if we don't realize it. If we cross our limits and harm Mother Nature, she will surely retaliate. We often forget how important we are and the significant roles we play. We think we are alone in the universe, but we are just at the beginning of discovering many answers. Even today, our knowledge of our own planet and its myriad species is limited. We don't even fully understand who we are or where we truly belong."

He paused, letting the enormity of his words sink in. The night sky, vast and unfathomable, seemed to echo his thoughts. "But in a race, we won and were chosen by nature to find answers to all these questions," Sam remarked, his voice filled with quiet conviction.

"It's not just about survival or making aname for ourselves. It's about discovery, about understanding the deeper connections that bind us to this universe."

George looked at Sam, curiosity piqued. "You're right, there are a lot of things we don't really know. But what do you mean by we 'think' we are the only ones in the universe? Do you think there are others?"

Sam turned his gaze back to the stars, his expression contemplative. "Maybe," he said, pausing thoughtfully. Then, with a smile, he asked George, "Do you really want to be alone in this endless universe?"

"Life doesn't have to be a creature with two legs, two arms, and one head. It can take any form. There are infinite possibilities in nature. The vastness of this universe holds countless options that we can't even begin to imagine. However, the distance between us and other potential life forms creates a gap between various universes. In a way, that's a good thing."

"Why safe?" George questioned.

"The levels of knowledge, thought processes, priorities, sense organs, and mindsets may differ completely from one another," Sam remarked. "Interacting with a completely different form of life might create unnecessary problems. The distance acts as a buffer, allowing each civilization to grow and evolve independently without interference."

He paused, allowing the vastness of the cosmos to underscore his words. "We just discussed that we're unaware of so many things, right? So may be we don't really know."

After a few seconds of contemplation, George replied, "You may be right. But I think those are just movie fantasies, Sam! There's no concrete evidence of such creatures. Oh God! What if they are bad and have no empathy, sympathy, or kindness? What if they destroy mankind?"

Sam smiled, his eyes reflecting the vastness of his imagination. "How can we decide if they are good or bad? Maybe they are both, depending on our perspective. Just like we coexist with other beings on this planet. If an eagle misses a fish during its hunt, we feel happy for the fish, even though the eagle is disappointed. Yet, the next morning, we might order fish fry at a restaurant." Sam burst into laughter, and George joined in.

He leaned back, gazing up at the

starlit sky. "The composition of life forms could vary vastly from place to place," he mused.

"Different elements might play crucial roles in the lives of beings. Some might exist as liquids, gases, or something else entirely."

Sam's thoughts ventured further into the realms of possibility. "Here on Earth, we have five specific elements and five sense organs. But in other universes, living beings might sense, eat, and listen with their skin, and speak with their ears. They might have more or fewer sense organs than we do." He laughed loudly at the thought, the sound echoing through the quiet night. "The composition of life out there could be far more complex and diverse than we can even imagine."

George chuckled, intrigued by Sam's vivid imagination. "That's quite a picture you're painting, Sam."

Sam's eyes twinkled with curiosity as he added, "On some planets, there might be no gender, and death might be completely different from what we know. And who knows," he said with a grin, "there might not be marriages or girlfriends."

George laughed heartily, the tension of the earlier conversation dissolving into amusement. "Well, that would solve a lot of problems, wouldn't it?"

Sam joined in the laughter, their shared humor creating a bond of camaraderie. "Exactly! And think about it— on some planets, the concept of 'life' itself might be entirely different. May be there are beings who live forever or who can transfer their consciousness into different forms."

George, thinking deeply, replied, "Yeah, that might be true! But, honestly, thinking about it too much makes me a bit uneasy. Let's change the topic."

George continued with a teasing grin, "By the way, you're so cool! How come you don't have a girlfriend?"

Sam laughed, shaking his head. "You're bored and diverting the topic. I don't know! We discussed some deep stuff and now we're back to talking about my non-existent girlfriend!"

George chuckled, but then his expression turned earnest. "Hey buddy, if you have anything to share or talk about, just remember I'm here for you."

Sam looked at George, a playful glint in his eye. "You definitely want to kiss me!" he teased, breaking into a grin.

Both of them burst out laughing, the shared humor easing the weight of their earlier conversation. The laughter was contagious, echoing under the night sky and lightening their spirits.

After the laughter subsided, George lay back on the grass, gazing up at the stars. "Seriously, though, Sam. You're one of the most insightful people I know. You have this magnetic personality. It's hard to believe you're still single."

Sam smiled, his eyes reflecting the stars above.

"I'm so sorry, guys!" Lisa exclaimed as

she arrived, slightly out of breath. "Professor Amit wanted to discuss something, so I couldn't postpone the conversation."

George's reassuring gesture, rubbing Lisa's shoulder, spoke volumes. "As expected... It's okay, Liz. Chill! Don't worry," he comforted her.

Lisa's surprised giggle broke through the tension. "Wait! Am I dreaming? I expected this response from Sam, not you. I thought you'd be pissed off!"

George adopted a mock-serious tone, his voice carrying a hint of mischief. "Oh, really! I'm a changed man now. What you did was aneye-opener for me."

Lisa's smile widened, her curiosity piqued. "Oh, is it? What did you learn?"

George's response was playful, yet tinged with humor. "Never wait for girls whose wrist watches count one second as one hour and are completely unpredictable. Especially not Lisa!" With a mischievous grin, he darted toward the hostel.

Lisa and Sam couldn't help but laugh, their earlier concerns momentarily forgotten in the joy of the moment. Their laughter echoed through the night as they ran after George, the bonds of friendship growing stronger with each shared moment.

* * * * *

4

"Hi, Sam!" George's sudden appearance made Sam startle slightly, his focus broken from whatever occupied his thoughts moments before.

"Hey... when did you come?" Sam asked, a touch of surprise evident in his voice as he shifted his attention to George. His sudden inquiry was accompanied by a subtle attempt to mask the slight fluster that had momentarily overtaken him.

"Just now, while you were murmuring. Were you talking to somebody?" George's curiosity was palpable, his eyes keen as he observed Sam's reaction, sensing something amiss.

"No. Of course," Sam replied and kept his mobile in his pocket. His tone striving for casualness, though a flicker of uncertainty betrayed his attempt to deflect attention.

George raised an eyebrow, detecting the hint of evasion in Sam's response. "I know. You've been talking to your girlfriend. I noticed, and now you're caught," he teased, a playful smirk playing at the corners of his lips as he gently teased Sam.

Sam felt a flush of embarrassment tinge his cheeks, his attempt to conceal his conversation now laid bare. Despite his efforts, he couldn't help but offer a sheepish smile, the awkwardness of the moment mingling with a sense of camaraderie as he continued the conversation.

"I always admire you, Sam," George said, looking at Sam with a praising expression.

"During yesterday's event, you could tell the exact number of people present without even head counting. How is that possible?" George expressed his surprise, his admiration evident in his tone.

"My guess is accurate to a maximum extent. I can consolidate as quickly as possible," Sam replied modestly, downplaying his remarkable skill.

"Could be. But it is not maximum. It is hundred percent accurate. I can't imagine this. It is something divine," George complimented, his awe palpable.

"Thanks for the compliment," Sam responded, feeling grateful for George's admiration, though he remained humble in his acknowledgment.

"Your accuracy always mesmerizes me. Your driving, presentation, response time, what not... everywhere you are unique," George continued, his admiration unwavering as he praised Sam's exceptional abilities.

"I already thanked you... No further stock is available... Let us go..." Sam gently interrupted, his hand resting on George's shoulder as he led the way back to the hostel. Despite the exchange coming to an end, the warmth of their conversation lingered between them, strengthening their bond as friends.

* * * * *

"By the way, Lisa, how was your submission?" Sam inquired as they walked, his genuine interest in her well-being evident in his tone.

"It was good, Sam. But I'm sorry once again, I convinced you to come out and then made you guys wait," Lisa frowned, expressing her regret, her concern for inconveniencing her friends apparent.

"It's okay, Lisa. Don't worry about it," Sam comforted her with a reassuring smile, his easy-going nature offering solace and understanding.

As Sam walked away while talking on his mobile, Lisa and George began to ascend the stairs, with Sam ahead of them. The scene unfolded with a sense of camaraderie and mutual support, each member of the group offering understanding and kindness to one another.

Lisa scrolled through her mobile, but suddenly slipped and lost her balance. Just as she was about to crumble to the ground, Sam returned to the stairs and saw her in distress. Reacting swiftly, he rushed towards her, his instincts kicking in to prevent her fall. With a deft movement, he grabbed herby the waist and turned her around, averting the accident.

However, in the process, Sam ended up hitting his face on the ground, a sharp pain shooting through his mouth.

"Are you okay, Sam?" Lisa screamed, hervoice filled with alarm as she rushed to his side, her concern evident in her expression.

"Sam, you're bleeding from your tooth. Oh God! Let's go to the medical room!" Lisa exclaimed, her voice trembling with emotion as tears welled up in her eyes, overwhelmed by worry for her friend's well-being. The unexpected turn of events underscored the bonds of care and support that united the group, prompting them to rally around Sam in his moment of need.

"What happened?" George asked in a hurry as he reached them, running, his concern evident in his voice and expression.

Lisa and Sam exchanged awkward

glances, unsure of how to explain the situation to George. Lisa began to recount the incident but stopped short, only mentioning the part where Sam had tried to save her, omitting the details of his injury.

"Let's go to the dentist," George insisted, his urgency reflecting his worry for Sam's well-being. However, Sam brushed it off, determined to handle the situation himself. With a calm demeanor, he wiped the blood with a handkerchief and washed his face and mouth at the washbasin, downplaying the severity of his injury.

"I'm okay now. Don't worry. No need for a doctor," Sam assured them, his voice steady despite the discomfort he must have been feeling.

"You're too insensitive. That's why girls don't like you," Lisa expressed, her voice tinged with disappointment and concern, tears welling up in her eyes. She looked at Sam, her emotions raw and vulnerable, hoping he would understand.

"Thank God... I'm free from all clutches and liberated," Sam laughed, his light-hearted tone contrasting with the gravity of the situation, seemingly unaffected by Lisa and George's emotional reactions.

* * * * *

5

"Yes, Doctor. For over six months now,"Lisa replied softly, her voice carrying a hint of vulnerability, revealing the weight of her burden.

"What are the other symptoms?" the physician inquired gently, his eyes filled with concern, reflecting his empathy for Lisa's plight.

Lisa paused, gathering her thoughts, her demeanour betraying the turmoil within her. "Daydreaming," she began, her words flowing like poetry, each syllable laden with emotion. "I drift between moments of exhilaration and euphoria, nights lost to sleeplessness, a hunger that refuses to be sated, trembling hands, a heart that races like a wild stallion and breaths that come in hurried gasps... These are the symptoms that haunt me," she explained, her voice trembling with the weight of her confession, baring her innermost struggles to the physician's compassionate gaze.

The physician nodded, his expression understanding, as he delved into the delicate matter with gentle curiosity. "Do you have a boyfriend?" he asked softly, his tone inviting honesty and openness.

"Of course," Lisa replied, her voice carrying a hint of bashfulness, her thoughts momentarily drifting to the special individuals who held her affections. The physician noticed subtle changes in Lisa's breathing and heartbeat as she spoke, even without a physical examination, sensing the depth of her emotions.

"How many?" the doctor prodded gently, a playful twinkle in his eye, inviting Lisa to share more about her romantic entanglements.

Lisa's cheeks flushed slightly as she admitted, "Only one," her voice carrying a mixture of fondness and vulnerability.

"Okay... When you suddenly face him, is there any difference in your heartbeat observed?" the doctor teased lightly, a soft chuckle escaping him, his demeanor warm andreassuring.

A blush deepened on Lisa's cheeks as she confessed, "Yes, Doctor. When I see Sam, my heart seems to dance to a melody only he can hear. Even now, it's the same..." Her admission was tinged with a mixture of affection and trepidation, her gaze flickering between the doctor and the door, as if unsure of what her feelings might lead to.

The physician's eyes crinkled with amusement as he posed his final question, his demeanor light-hearted yet perceptive. "And when someone else spends time with him, do you feel a pang of jealousy?" he asked with a knowing smile, inviting Lisa to explore her emotions with honesty and introspection.

Lisa's laughter bubbled forth, a joyful expression of her innermost feelings as she acknowledged the complexities of her heart. "Yes, of course," she replied, her voice filled with a mixture of amusement and affection.

The physician's laughter joined hers, the sound echoing through the room like a melody of understanding and acceptance.

"There is no need for medicine now. One free piece of advice: follow your heart and speak your truth," he concluded, his words carrying a sense of wisdom and whimsy, leaving Lisa feeling reassured and empowered to navigate the intricacies of her emotions.

* * * * *

6

"Can't believe it's already been a year. We have to leave now, and you have another three months," exclaimed George, his gaze fixed on Sam with a hint of disbelief.

"Sam, this is our last week in this college, with you!" gasped Riya, her voice tinged with sadness. "It's hard to imagine not seeing you every day."

"Yes, I can't believe you will be leaving next week, guys," replied Sam, looking at Lisa with a mixture of fondness and melancholy. "I'll miss our late-night study sessions and all the fun we had."

"Okay, enough sadness. I think we should plan a trip together and make it memorable for Sam and us. Any suggestions?" George suggested, trying to lift the mood. His eyes sparkled with anticipation.

"What about the Taj Mahal?" Riya suggested eagerly, her eyes lighting up. "I've always wanted to see it, and it's such aromantic place!"

"Perfect! I'm down. What about others?" George asked, seeking approval from the group.

Everyone nodded their heads and gave thumbs up in agreement, their spirits lifted by the prospect of the trip.

"Okay, guys, then let's finalize this plan. After the trip, we all can leave directly from there except Sam," George explained his plan to the group, determination shining in his eyes. "It'll be the perfect way to end our time together."

"Yes! We should definitely visit the Taj Mahal at sunrise," Lisa chimed in. "I've heard it's absolutely breath taking, and we can take some amazing pictures."

"And we can explore Agra Fort too," Riya added, excitement coloring her voice. "There's so much history there!"

"Don't forget about trying the local cuisine," Sam said, a smile playing on his lips. "I've heard Agra is famous for its petha and Mughlai food. We can have a feast!"

George, taking charge, started making notes on his phone. "Alright, I'll book the flight tickets and look for a decent place to stay near the Taj. Let's make this trip unforgettable."

As they continued planning, the sadness of impending separation was replaced by the anticipation of one last adventure together. Their laughter and chatter filled the air, creating memories even before the trip began. The promise of the Taj Mahal trip served as a beacon of joy, a testament to their friendship and the beautiful moments they had shared over the past year.

The Taj Mahal, nestled on the banks of the sacred Yamuna River, stands as a timeless symbol of love and architectural brilliance. This majestic monument, with its gleaming white marble and intricate carvings, draws millions of visitors from around the world. However, the allure of this place extends beyond its stunning facade.

The Yamuna River, winding gracefully past the Taj Mahal, is steeped in history and divinity. According to Hindu mythology, these very banks cradled the childhood of Lord Krishna, the beloved deity known for his playful and miraculous deeds. It is said that the young Krishna's laughter once echoed through the flourishing groves that bordered the river and his divine love stories with Radha unfolded along these sacred waters.

The riverbanks here are not merely geographical features; they are hallowed grounds where tales of divine love and devotion have resonated through the ages. This sense of sanctity, coupled with the rich tapestry of legends surrounding the Yamuna, infuses the Taj Mahal with an even deeper spiritual significance. Visitors who come to marvel at the Taj Mahal's unparalleled beauty often find themselves moved by the profound sense of history and holiness that pervades the entire area.

Standing on the riverbanks, one can almost hear the ancient whispers of

Krishna's flute and feel the timeless romance that the Taj Mahal so poignantly embodies. It is a place where the past and present intertwine seamlessly, where every stone and every ripple in the river speaks of a legacy of love that transcends time.

Apart from the ancient love story of Radha and Krishna associated with the Yamuna River, there is also the poignant historical tale of Mumtaz and Shah Jahan connected to the Taj Mahal. Shah Jahan constructed this magnificent monument in loving memory of his beloved wife, Mumtaz.

The entire team reached their hotel in Delhi, the bustling capital of India, with an air of excitement and anticipation. They had chosen a hotel conveniently located close to the road leading to Agra, the city that houses the Taj Mahal. The plan was to rest briefly and then set out early in the morning to witness the dawn at one of the world's most iconic monuments.

As the group settled into their rooms, the energy was palpable. They chatted animatedly about the journey ahead, discussing the history and beauty of the Taj Mahal. However, their excitement was tempered by a minor hiccup in their plans.

George, who had been eagerly looking forward to the trip, was struck by a suddenbout of stomach upset. His face was pale, and he managed a weak smile as he addressed his friends. "You guys go ahead," he insisted, his voice slightly strained. "I'll catch up with you soon. I just need to rest for a bit."

The group gathered around George, their concern evident. "Are you sure you'll be okay?" Lisa asked, her brow furrowed withworry.

"Yeah, just give me some time to recover," George replied, trying to sound reassuring despite his discomfort. "I don't want you all to miss out on the sunrise at theTaj Mahal because of me."

Understanding his plight, the rest of the group nodded. They knew how much this trip meant to him, and they didn't want him to feel left out. "Alright, George," Sam said, patting him on the back. "We'll head out now, but make sure you join us as soon as you feel better. We won't start exploring until you get there."

With that, the group gathered their belongings and headed out, their excitement rekindled by the thought of the magnificent sight that awaited them. As they boarded the bus to Agra, they couldn't help but feel a mix of anticipation and sympathy for George.

Meanwhile, George rested in his hotel room, determined to join his friends as soon as he felt well enough. He knew he couldn't miss out on the experience of a lifetime, and the thought of standing before the Taj Mahal with his friends motivated him to recover quickly.

The journey to Agra was filled with chatter and laughter, the group's spirits high despite George's absence. They shared stories and snacks, their excitement growing with each passing kilometer. As they neared Agra, the silhouette of the Taj Mahal began to emerge on the horizon, its ethereal beauty promising a memorable day ahead.

Arriving at the gates of the Taj Mahal just as the first light of dawn began to break, the group paused for a moment, taking in the awe-inspiring view. They were ready to create unforgettable memories, and they knew George would join them soon to share in the magic of this remarkable journey.

"The Taj Mahal is an ivory-white marble mausoleum built by the Emperor Shah Jahan in the 17th century in memory of his beloved wife Mumtaz Mahal," the guide explained, his voice resonating with reverence. "Construction began in 1632 and took approximately 22 years to complete, with the help of around 20,000 artisans. This magnificent structure is often referred to as the 'Crown of the Palace' and is a symbol of eternal love."

He continued, "The Taj Mahal is not just a monument of love; it is a masterpiece of architectural innovation and design. Shah Jahan commissioned the Taj Mahal following the death of Mumtaz

Mahal during childbirth in 1631. The construction involved the expertise of craftsmen from across the empire and beyond, including calligraphers from Syria and Iran, inlayers from southern India, stonecutters from Baluchistan, and a specialist in building the central dome from Turkey."

The guide paused, allowing the group to absorb the grandeur of the sight before them. The sun had just begun to rise, casting a golden hue over the marble edifice and reflecting off the tranquil waters of the surrounding gardens. The Taj Mahal stood majestic and serene, its minarets reaching towards the heavens, encapsulating the love story that had inspired its creation.

As they continued their tour, the guide shared more details about the intricate craftsmanship. "The Taj Mahal's architecture is a fusion of Islamic, Persian, Ottoman Turkish, and Indian architectural styles. The mausoleum itself is built on a symmetrical plan, with an emphasis on bilateral symmetry along a central axis.

The central dome, which rises to about 73 meters, is surrounded by four smaller domes and four minarets, each standing at a height of about 40 meters. These minarets were designed slightly outward to protect the main tomb in case of an earthquake."

He pointed to the delicate inlay work, explaining, "The intricate floral designs and calligraphy you see are made using a technique called pietra dura, where semi-precious stones like lapis lazuli, turquoise, and jade are inlaid into the white marble. The inscriptions you see are verses from the Quran, intricately carved into the marble, adding a spiritual dimension to this architectural marvel."

"The gardens that surround the Taj Mahal are inspired by Persian gardens, known as Charbagh. These gardens are divided into four main parts, symbolizing the four rivers of Paradise. The long reflecting pool that stretches from the main gateway to the base of the tomb perfectly mirrors the beauty of the Taj, enhancing its ethereal beauty."

The guide's stories and facts deepened their appreciation for the Taj Mahal's beauty and the dedication that went into its creation. He shared the poignant history, mentioning how Shah Jahan was later deposed by his own son Aurangzeb and spent his last years imprisoned in the Agra Fort, gazing wistfully at the Taj Mahal, where his beloved Mumtaz lay.

Standing in the presence of such timeless beauty, the group felt a profound connection to the past and a sense of wonder at the enduring power of love that could inspire such an extraordinary feat of architecture.

With a twinkle in his eye, the guide added with a laugh, "It is an appropriate place to propose. Many couples from around the world choose this spot to express their love and commitment, drawn by the romantic history and breath-taking beauty of the Taj Mahal."

Lisa's eyes glowed with a sudden brightness as she stood mesmerized by the grandeur of the Taj Mahal. She was lost in another world, her thoughts drifting to the possibilities the guide's words had conjured. The romance and history of the place seemed to cast a spell on her.

Sam, however, seemed immune to the enchantment. "Do you know?" he began, his voice breaking through her reverie. "It took 22 years for 20,000 artisans and cost the equivalent of 1 billion US dollars to build."

"Great," Lisa replied, feeling a bit disheartened. Her thoughts had been far from statistics, and Sam's matter-of-fact response didn't align with the romantic sentiments she had been entertaining. She had envisioned stories of love and devotion, not the cold hard facts of construction costs and labor.

She tried to steer the conversation back to what she truly wanted to express. "Love made it possible," she said softly, her voice filled with a longing to connect with the deeper meaning behind the monument.

Sam remained unyielding, his face blank and unreadable. "Maybe," he replied. "But nothing remains."

Lisa looked at him, puzzled. "What do you mean?" she asked, hoping to understand his perspective.

Sam sighed, glancing at the Taj Mahal with a mixture of admiration and skepticism. "Love made it possible, yes," he said slowly. "But in the end, it's just a monument. The people who inspired it are gone. Time erases everything. Even love, eventually."

His words hung in the air, heavy with a melancholy truth that Lisa found hard to accept. She wanted to believe in the everlasting power of love, the idea that something as beautiful as the Taj Mahal could be a testament to love that never fades.

"But the Taj Mahal still stands," Lisa argued gently. "It's a symbol of their love. It's a reminder that something beautiful can endure even after the people are gone."

Sam nodded, conceding her point. "True," he said. "It's a symbol. But symbols can only carry so much. The real challenge is living up to those ideals in our own lives. To make our own love stories last."

Lisa smiled, feeling a bit better. "Maybe that's what makes it all worth it," she said. "The effort we put into love, knowing it might not last forever, but choosing to believe in it anyway."

Sam looked at her, his expression softening. "May be you're right," he admitted. "May be that's what makes it beautiful."

Their conversation trailed off as they continued to walk through the gardens, the majestic Taj Mahal standing tall behind them, a timeless reminder of the complexities and enduring power of love.

Gathering her courage by evening, Lisa looked directly at Sam, her heart pounding in her chest. She took a deep breath and said, "Sam, I would like to say something to you. Can't we continue our journey till the end?"

Sam remained silent, his expression unchanged, leaving Lisa in a moment of anxious anticipation. She could feel the weight of her words hanging in the air, a fragile bridge between them. Her mind raced with thoughts, each second stretching into what felt like aneternity.

"I am not kidding. I am serious and firm on my decision," Lisa repeated her voice steady but filled with emotion. Her eyes conveyed stories that words couldn't capture, filled with memories of shared laughter, deep conversations, and quiet moments of understanding.

She gazed into Sam's eyes, hoping to see a flicker of response, some sign that he understood the depth of her feelings.

The seconds ticked by slowly. Sam's silence was a chasm she desperately wanted to cross. Her eyes glistened with unspoken emotions, reflecting the warmth rising within her—a mixture of hope and anxiety, love and fear. She felt vulnerable, yet she knew that this moment was crucial.

Lisa continued to look at Sam, her heart in her throat. "We've been through so much together," she said softly. "And I believe that we can face whatever comes our way. I want us to face it together."

Sam was puzzled, his brow furrowed in deep thought. He couldn't meet Lisa's gaze, a clear sign of his inner turmoil. It was evident that he struggled to contain his feelings, his usual composure slipping away under the weight of Lisa's unexpected confession. The moonlight cast a soft glow around them, illuminating the tension in the air and making the moment almost unbearably tense.

"Lisa, my future is uncertain," Sam began, his voice tinged with hesitation and vulnerability. "How can we marry? I have so much to accomplish, so many dreams to pursue. Can't we remain friends?" His words came out in a rush, betraying the emotions swirling within him. He couldn't maintain eye contact, his gaze drifting to the full moon hanging in the sky, seemingly observing their exchange with silent curiosity.

The conversation felt jarringly out of sync with the romantic ambiance of the Taj Mahal and the serene night sky.

Lisa was stunned, her heart sinking as Sam's words echoed in her mind. Tears welled up in her eyes, spilling over despite her efforts to control them. She struggled to process Sam's hesitancy, feeling the weight of his refusal and the ache of her unreciprocated love.

"Please tell me one reason for your refusal," Lisa pleaded, her voice trembling with emotion. "Am I not meeting your requirements? Are you in love with somebody else? There should not be any chance to repent in the future, Sam. Mine is true love." She searched desperately for answers in his eyes, hoping to find solace in his response.

Sam's heart clenched at Lisa's words, his own emotions swirling within him. "Please understand," he began his voice steady but heavy with emotion. "I have dreams, and my parents also have certain expectations. I have to make them a reality. I don't want to tie my hands with any relations." His words were sincere, yet they offered little comfort to Lisa's aching heart.

"Let us start a new journey. I will be with you. I promise I won't be a hindrance," Lisa implored, her voice filled with determination and hope, clinging to the possibility of a future together.

Sam remained silent for a few moments, grappling with his inner turmoil. When he finally turned back, he saw George staring at him with a mixture of curiosity and concern. Lisa had already left, her figure fading into the distance, leaving behind a sense of emptiness and regret.

As Sam watched her go, his heart heavy with the weight of his decision, he couldn't shake the feeling that he had just turned away from something that could have been beautiful. The moonlight cast a soft glow on the majestic Taj Mahal, a silent witness to their parting and the bittersweet emotions that lingered in its shadow.

But in the grand scheme of life, seasons changed, and years passed, carrying with them the memories of that fateful night at the iconic monument of love.

* * * * *

7

"Hi George, how have you been?" Lisa's warm voice rang out through the phone, carrying a hint of nostalgia and genuine curiosity.

"Hey Lisa, it's been ages! I've been good, just busy with work. How about you? Did you manage to land that dream job at the news agency in New York?" George's voice crackled with excitement, eager to catch upwith an old friend.

"Yes, George! I did! It's been a whirlwind of excitement and learning. I'm absolutely loving it," Lisa shared animatedly, her voice alive with enthusiasm and satisfaction. "And what about you? Any big news on your end?"

"Funny you should ask. Brace yourself for a surprise," George replied, a mischievous edge in his tone. "I've actually landed a gig at SONAI Company. Looks like I'll be moving to New York next week."

"Wow, George! That's fantastic news!

SONAI is a top-notch company.

Congratulations!" Lisa exclaimed genuinely, her excitement evident even through the phone. "And did you have any inside connections or recommendations?"

"Believe it or not, Lisa, it was all on my own merit. Hard work pays off, you know," George boasted, a sense of pride seeping into his voice. "I'll be touching down in New York next week. Let's catch up before I dive into the new gig."

"Absolutely! It'll be great to see you, George. I hope you haven't changed too much," Lisa quipped playfully, her laughter echoing through the line.

"Not a chance! Same old George," he reassured her with a chuckle. "But hey, here's the kicker - Sam's the CEO at SONAI. How about we surprise him together?"

Lisa's tone shifted slightly, a mixture of surprise and reservation creeping in. "I know... He's really made strides in his career."

"Would you be up for joining me when we meet him?" George pressed, eager for her company in what promised to be a memorable reunion.

"Of course! And I've got a little surprise of my own for him," Lisa responded with a smile, her voice laced with intrigue and anticipation.

* * * * *

8

"Sam, a program about you is being telecasted on the ANN channel," the secretary informed Sam through the intercom, her voice tinged with excitement.

Sam's curiosity piqued, he quickly switched on the television, his anticipation building as he waited for the program about his career to begin. As the segment unfolded, he found himself drawn into the narrative, eager to see how his journey would be portrayed.

"Sam, CEO of SONAI, one of the top 500 Fortune Companies, who allocates 80% of his wage to eco-friendly programs," the announcer's voice boomed through the speakers, filling the room with a sense of pride. "He is a philanthropist, known for his dynamic leadership and as one of the youngest CEOs in the world. He is a fervent advocate for corporate social responsibility."

As the program delved deeper into

Sam's background, detailing his rise to success from humble beginnings, Sam couldn't help but reflect on his journey. Memories of his father, Ramson, toiling away in their small village in India flooded his mind, reminding him of the sacrifices made to reach his current position.

"His father, Ramson, was a farmer in a remote village of India. Samson completed his high school education there and has risen to this prestigious level," the program continued, painting a vivid picture of Sam's upbringing and the challenges he had overcome along the way.

Images of Sam's childhood home and school flashed across the screen, transporting him back to a time when life was simpler yet filled with dreams of a brighter future. The voices of his childhood friends, sharing fond memories and anecdotes, added a personal touch to the narrative, reminding Sam of the bonds forged in his youth.

As the program drew to a close, Sam found himself filled with a sense of pride and gratitude. Despite the challenges and obstacles, he had faced, he had persevered,and his journey had led him to this moment of recognition and acclaim.

"Please find out who the reporter is," Sam requested his secretary through the intercom, a sense of curiosity tingling withinhim.

"Sure," the secretary replied promptly, disappearing to gather the information.

Moments later, the secretary returnedwith news of unexpected visitors. "Sir, Ms. Lisa and Mr. George want to meet you," she announced.

Surprised and delighted, Sam hurriedly exited his office room, a warm smile already forming on his face as he anticipated their reunion.

As Sam approached Lisa and George in the reception area, he couldn't contain his excitement, enveloping them both in tight embraces.

With a playful glint in her eye, Lisa teased, "This time you can't escape," prompting a chuckle from Sam.

Returning her banter with a grin, Sam quipped, "Neither can you."

The reunion filled Sam with a wave of nostalgia, evoking memories of their time together on campus. "What a pleasant surprise. You guys never change. Just like back on campus. I've missed you all these days," he confessed, a hint of emotion coloring his words.

As George began recounting stories from their time apart, the atmosphere became light-hearted, filled with laughter andshared memories.

Sam's smile widened at the thought of catching up over dinner at his place later that evening. "Can't we catch up on all of this over dinner at my place this evening? My father is also with me, and I'd love to introduce you guys to him," he suggested warmly.

George's revelation about his recent appointment only added to the excitement. "Sure, and from today, we can even have lunch together," he chimed in, his enthusiasm palpable.

Surprised by George's decision to join him, Sam couldn't help but express his gratitude. "I had no idea you were joining me. Please be part of my personal team and help me out. I have some plans," he requested earnestly.

George's response was immediate and enthusiastic. "It's my pleasure, Sam. I'm in, absolutely," he affirmed, his commitment unwavering.

* * * * *

9

Sam greeted Lisa and George at the portico with a warm smile, his eyes reflecting genuine happiness at their presence.

"I'm so happy to see both of you at the same time," Sam expressed sincerely, his voice tinged with emotion, conveying the depth of his feelings.

As they settled into their seats, they began to reminisce about their college days, sharing stories and laughter over glasses of wine.

"Finally, you've become an investigative journalist. This profession suits you perfectly. Your program is excellent and really delves deep," Sam complimented Lisa, his admiration evident in his tone as they savored their drinks.

"Yeah, that's me... I'm spying on you... and not just you..." Lisa joked, injecting a playful tone into the conversation, her eyes sparkling with mischief.

Sam beamed proudly at Lisa's wit, feeling a sense of pride in her achievements as he led her and George to meet his father, Ramson, who awaited them on the first floor.

"Dad, these are my friends, Lisa and George," Sam introduced them with a touch of reverence, his voice carrying a note of respect.

Both Lisa and George extended warm greetings to Ramson, acknowledging the aura of authority and wisdom that surrounded him. Ramson carried himself with the air of a disciplined college principal, his presence commanding respect and admiration. Behind his subtle expressions lay a wealth of experience and knowledge, evident in the twinkle of wisdom that flickered in his eyes.

"Sam has told me about your journey. You're truly remarkable, going from where you started to where you are now. It's truly amazing," Lisa complimented, her voice full of admiration.

"It's been quite the journey," Ramson

responded, his eyes crinkling at the corners as he smiled warmly. "Sam mentioned that you've done quite a bit of research on me and my son."

"Yeah, I was fascinated by your story," Lisa replied. "I wanted to know more about you. In fact, I was considering conducting a personal interview with you before airing the program. But I was a bit hesitant, and I didn't want Sam to find out before it was broadcast," she added with a laugh, her eyes sparkling with mischief.

"What's so great about me? I lived in a remote village in India. There, I managed to earn a good reputation and command some respect. Sam's childhood was spent there as well. Slowly, he made his way to Kolkata, and we followed him," Ramson explained, a hint of nostalgia in his smile. His voice carried the weight of many years andexperiences.

"Yes, absolutely. I've visited those locations. They're surrounded by deep forests with rare species of plants. It must have been incredibly beautiful. You were so lucky to spend so much time there," Lisa complimented, her voice filled with genuine admiration and a hint of wistfulness, perhaps reflecting her own longing for such experiences.

"It was indeed a beautiful place," Ramson said, his eyes distant as he recalled his past. "The forests, the simplicity of life, and the close-knit community. It was a different world altogether. We had our challenges, but it was home."

"Sam often spoke about those times with such fondness," Lisa added, looking at Sam with a smile. "It seems like those early experiences shaped him into the person he is today."

"Absolutely," Ramson agreed, nodding. "Those experiences instilled in him a sense of resilience and determination. He saw first-hand the value of hard work and the importance of staying true to one's roots."

"And now look at where he is," George chimed in, his voice filled with pride. "Leading a top Fortune 500 company and making sucha significant impact."

Sam smiled, feeling a mixture of prideand humility as he listened to the conversation. The room was filled with a sense of camaraderie and shared history, the bonds of friendship and family interwoven withevery word spoken.

Sam then led Lisa and George to a special room filled with an impressive book collection he and his father had amassed over the years. It was akin to the British Museum, with a vast array of collections covering every imaginable subject. The books were meticulously arranged, each one alphabetically sorted by subject. It was like gazing up at the glittering stars in a clear night sky – truly awe-inspiring. Lisa couldn't contain her excitement at the sight of such an extensive and well-organized collection.

"This is incredible, Sam. I had no idea you had such a treasure trove of knowledge here," Lisa exclaimed, her eyes wide with wonder as she scanned the shelves.

"I have a variety of collections in my house. I never restricted myself to books," Ramson explained, his pride evident in his voice. "I've always believed in the importance of a broad education and exposure to different subjects and ideas."

"I noticed that. Your ambiance is truly something out of this world," Lisa complimented, her admiration clear. She ran her fingers gently along the spines of the books, feeling the history and knowledge they contained.

"Thank you, Lisa," Ramson replied, smiling warmly. "I've preached the same to Sam as well. I hope he'll fulfil my dreams, of course, not alone, but with the help of his teams and friends like you."

"We'll do our best to support him," George added, his voice filled with determination. "It's clear that this legacy of learning and growth is something special, and we'll do everything we can to help Sam continue it."

"Absolutely," Lisa agreed, nodding.

"It's inspiring to see how much you both value knowledge and education. It's no wonder Samhas achieved so much."

Sam felt a deep sense of gratitude as he listened to the conversation. "I've learnedso much from my father," he said, his voice filled with emotion. "His wisdom and guidance have been invaluable to me, and I know I wouldn't be where I am today without his influence."

"We're lucky to have such a strong foundation," Ramson said, placing a hand on Sam's shoulder. "And with friends like you both, I have no doubt that Sam will continueto grow and achieve great things."

Ramson emphasized the importance of responsible development, stating with a thoughtful tone, "Development doesn't entail the destruction of the ecosystem. True progress doesn't come from overruling and exploiting other species for our own gain, whether that means killing them for consumption or using them recklessly for our purposes. Instead, it's essential to recognize the intrinsic value of all life forms. Each species, no matter how small or seemingly insignificant, plays a vital role in maintaining the delicate balance of nature."

He continued, his voice filled with conviction, "We must cherish the rare opportunity of embodying consciousness and being a living being on this planet. Our actions should reflect our understanding of this privilege and our duty to preserve it for future generations. This means making mindful choices that support sustainability and environmental stewardship."

Pausing for a moment to let his words sink in, Ramson added, "Despite our technological advancements, humans are still in a stage of infancy when it comes to our relationship with the natural world. We possess many tools and resources, but if not managed wisely, they may lead to our own downfall rather than genuine progress. We need to develop a sense of responsibility and foresight, ensuring that our innovations do not come at the cost of the environment and the myriad of life forms that share this Earth with us."

Lisa and George listened intently, clearly moved by Ramson's wisdom. "Your perspective is incredibly insightful, Mr. Ramson," Lisa said, her voice filled with respect. "It's a powerful reminder of the responsibilities we have as stewards of this planet. Your approach to development is something we should all strive to adopt in our personal and professional lives."

George nodded in agreement. "Absolutely. It's easy to get caught up in the rush of technological progress and economic growth, but hearing you speak about the importance of ecological balance and sustainability brings everything into perspective. I feel inspired to contribute more actively to preserving our environment."

Ramson smiled, pleased to see the impact his words had on the younger generation. "Thank you, both of you. It's heartening to see such enthusiasm and commitment to making a positive difference. Remember, every small action counts, and together, we can create a future where progress and preservation go hand in hand."

The conversation continued with a renewed sense of purpose, the room filled with a shared determination to make a meaningful impact on the world around them.

As George and Ramson enjoyed their drinks by the poolside, Ramson remarked with a smile, "You know, my drinking is fairly well under control these days. A glass or two nowand then helps me unwind."

George, however, was feeling the effects of his drinks much more strongly. He laughed, albeit a bit unsteadily, and admitted,"Well, I can't say the same for myself right now. It seems I've gone a bit overboard," he said, his words slurring slightly.

Meanwhile, Lisa and Sam sat on the edge of the pool, their legs playfully splashing the water as they reminisced about their college days. The sound of their laughter filled the air, mingling with the gentle lapping of the water against the pool's edge.

"Do you still practice yoga, Lisa?" Sam asked, genuinely curious. "I remember you were so dedicated back in college. It always seemed to bring you so much peace and energy."

Lisa smiled warmly at the memory. "Yes, I do. Yoga has been a constant in my life, no matter where I am or what I'm doing. It's helped me stay grounded and focused, especially during the more hectic times."

"And what about that adventurous short film you made? The one where you travelled to all those remote places?" Sam continued, his interest piqued.

"Oh, that was quite the journey," Lisa replied, her eyes sparkling with enthusiasm. "After I left India, I pursued journalism courses out of sheer passion. It was during one of my assignments that I got the idea for the short film. I wanted to capture the essence of adventure and the beauty of untouched landscapes."

She paused, then continued, "Joining the ANN News agency was a turning point.

My boss saw potential in me and suggested that I make short films on successful entrepreneurs. That's when I started to notice the common traits among the young CEOs I interviewed. They all had this incredible drive and vision, but also a deep respect for their roots and a commitment togiving back to society."

Sam listened intently, fascinated by her journey. "That's amazing, Lisa. It sounds likeyou've found a way to combine your love for story telling with making a real impact."

Lisa nodded. "It's been fulfilling, Sam. Meeting all these inspiring individuals has taught me so much. And it's funny, in a way, it brought me back to you. I mean, here you are, a successful CEO with a vision for a better world. It's like coming full circle."

Sam looked thoughtful for a moment. "I guess it is. And I'm glad we reconnected, Lisa. It's been too long."

The two friends continued to share stories, their bond growing stronger with each word exchanged, while George and Ramson's laughter echoed from the poolside, adding to the warmth of the reunion.

Suddenly, they heard a loud splash as Ramson slipped into the pool. Panic surged through the group. Without hesitation, Lisa quickly jumped in, followed closely by Sam. Together, they pulled Ramson out of the water, Lisa's heart pounding with adrenaline as she immediately began administering firstaid.

"Ramson, can you hear me?" Lisa called out, her voice steady despite her worry.

Ramson coughed and sputtered, struggling to regain his breath. Lisa worked quickly and efficiently, her training evident in her swift actions.

"Don't worry, Lisa. He'll be alright. Let me take care of it," Sam reassured her, gently but firmly taking over the situation. He didn't want her to bear the burden alone.

Disappointed at not being able to help

further, Lisa stepped back, watching as Sam lifted his father effortlessly and carried him to his bedroom. She felt like a stranger in that moment, her sense of helplessness contrasting sharply with Sam's calm control.

George, already in a hangover-induced haze, looked around blearily, barely comprehending what was happening. "Is everything okay?" he slurred, struggling to stand up.

Sam returned from the bedroom, his face etched with concern but relief. "He's alright now," he confirmed, wiping a stray drop of water from his brow. "He just needs some rest. He swallowed a bit of water, but he'll be fine."

Lisa let out a breath she didn't realize she had been holding. "Thank God," she murmured, feeling a mixture of relief and fear." Her words carried a hint of grateful that things hadn't turned out worse.

Sam placed a reassuring hand on her shoulder. "You did great, Lisa. Your quick actions helped a lot. We all have our roles, and sometimes, it's just about being there."

George, swaying slightly, tried to focus on the conversation. "Glad he's okay," he mumbled, his words barely coherent.

Sam chuckled softly, shaking his head at his friend's state. "Come on, George. Let'sget you to bed too. It's been quite a night."

As Sam helped George to his feet, Lisa felt a strange mix of emotions. She was grateful for Sam's strength and leadership but also felt an unfamiliar distance growing between them. The night had taken an unexpected turn, and as they settled back into the house, the earlier joy of their reunion was tinged with a new, sobering reality.

* * * * *

10

Lisa rushed into her boss's office, her face etched with urgency. "I need to talk toyou privately and urgently," she said, her tone leaving no room for doubt.

CEO Henry looked up from his paperwork, sensing the seriousness in her voice. "What's going on?" he asked, his curiosity piqued but his tone calm.

"Privately," Lisa repeated, her eyes scanning the room to emphasize the need for confidentiality.

Understanding the gravity of the situation, Henry gestured for his colleagues to leave the room. They exchanged curious glances but complied quickly, sensing that something important was about to unfold. Once the door clicked shut, Henry turned his full attention to Lisa.

"What's going on?" he asked again, thistime his concern more apparent.

Lisa leaned forward, lowering her

voice to a near whisper. "There's something fishy," she said urgently, her eyes darting around as if to ensure no one was eavesdropping.

"Regarding what?" Henry's irritation was evident now, his patience wearing thin. "You need to be more specific, Lisa."

"You instructed me to prepare similar stories of successful young CEOs of Fortune 500 companies," Lisa began, noticing the curiosity growing on her boss's face. "But there's something peculiar about a few of these CEOs or heads of major companies who reached that position at a young age."

Henry leaned forward, his interest piqued. "Go on," he prompted.

Lisa took a marker pen and walked to the whiteboard, writing down her observations as she spoke. "I've identified several commonalities among them," she said. She wrote:

1.   SON families occupy key positions.

2.   They prioritize nature.

3. They support eco-friendly projects exclusively.

4. Their HR department actively participates in similar activities.

5. They abstain from anti-ecological projects.

6. They prefer solitude, even during leisure.

7. They hail from remote village backgrounds.

8. Their abilities, resilience, and sustainability surpass those of theaverage person.

Henry's eyebrows furrowed as he read the list. "What's so remarkable or unique about that?" he asked coolly. "I also appreciate nature. Your generation constantly lectures and advocates, yet you're the most affected by excessive materialistic development. This could simply be coincidental and expected, as the younger generation must rectify the mistakes made by our predecessors."

"There's more," Lisa continued,

addinganother point to the board:

9.   They are unmarried.

Henry smirked, "Do you want anyone to get married to you?" Seeing the anger on Lisa's face, he quickly became serious. "Just kidding," he added, raising his hands in mocksurrender.

Lisa's expression hardened as she continued, "And they have gold teeth."

Henry showing some curiosity for the first time during the discussion, leaned forward and asked, "Gold teeth? That's an interesting detail. Is there any significance to that?"

Lisa nodded, her eyes serious. "Yes, it's a peculiar pattern I noticed among a few of these CEOs. They have gold teeth."

Henry furrowed his brows, processing the information. "That is indeed intriguing. But what could be the reason behind it?"

Lisa shrugged, her eyes narrowing thoughtfully. "I believe these aren't just gold teeth; they're transmitters, or tooth mics."

Henry's eyebrows shot up in surprise, his eyes widening in disbelief. "What do youmean? Transmitters?"

"I'm not sure yet," Lisa admitted, a hintof frustration creeping into her voice. "But it seems too specific to be a coincidence. These gold teeth might be a way for them to communicate or monitor things discreetly."

Henry's face paled slightly at the implications. "If that's true, then we may bedealing with something far more complex thanwe initially thought."

Lisa nodded grimly. "Exactly. That's why we need to investigate further and find out what they're hiding."

Henry leaned forward, his expression serious and concerned. "What's the plan, then?" he interjected, his tone more seriousnow.

Lisa squared her shoulders, determination etched on her face. "I'll come up with one," she said confidently.

"First, I'll need to gather more evidence and try to verify. We can't afford to tip them off that we're onto them."

Henry nodded slowly, still processing the gravity of the situation. "Alright, but be careful, Lisa. If there's a powerful network behind this, it could be dangerous."

"I understand," Lisa replied, her voice steady. "But we can't ignore this. If there's a conspiracy involving these CEOs, we need to expose it."

As she turned to leave, Henry called after her, a note of caution in his voice, "Remember, Lisa, if things go south, it could mean the end of the office. We have to tread carefully."

Lisa paused at the door, her resolve unwavering. "Don't worry, Henry. I'll be careful," she promised. "But this is too important to ignore. we need to get to the bottom of this."

Henry watched her go, a mix of worry and admiration on his face. After she disappeared from sight, he took out his mobile and made a call, giving concise instructions in a hushed tone. His expression conveyed a sense of urgency, hinting at the gravity of the situation he was addressing.

Lisa's determination was clear, and he knew she wouldn't back down. As she exited the room, she felt a renewed sense of purpose, determined to unravel the mystery surrounding the enigmatic SON executives and their unusual gold teeth.

* * * * *

11

"George, can we meet this evening?" Lisa requested, her voice carrying a sense of urgency.

"Done. At Odeon," George replied without hesitation.

When they met in the cozy corner of Odeon, George noticed the anxiety in Lisa's eyes. "What's the hurry? You look so anxious," he questioned, raising an eyebrow as he flagged down a waiter and ordered French onion soup for them both.

Lisa took a deep breath, trying to organize her thoughts. "There are some strange things I've noticed about Sam... Not just Sam, but also many other successful entrepreneurs," she began, her voice tense. She then explained in detail the peculiar patterns and coincidences she had previously narrated to her boss, including the gold teeth and their potential significance.

George listened, his face a mix of skepticism and curiosity. He shook his head slowly and commented, "It sounds accidental. I can't believe that," while simultaneously glancing at his mobile, checking messages.

Lisa couldn't control her anger and shook George's shoulder, shouting, "Do you think I'm mad? Can't you understand the gravity of what I'm saying? This is a matter of life and death. You must cooperate with me!"

George looked puzzled, taken aback by her intensity. "It goes against my principles, Lisa. I can't. I work under Sam. You should understand that," he replied, trying to remain calm but clearly uncomfortable.

Lisa stepped closer, her eyes boring into his. "Have you not noticed the strange behavior of Sam and his father?" she demanded. "The way they act, the things they say... Don't you find any of it odd?"

George averted his gaze, his discomfort growing. "I can't say anything about it, Lisa. Let's just go," he said, his voice wavering ashe started to stand up.

Lisa's frustration reached a boiling point. "Now I understand. You're also in cahoots," she remarked bitterly, her voicedripping with accusation.

George stopped in his tracks and turnedback to face her. "In cahoots? Are you serious?" he asked, his tone a mix of disbelief and hurt. "You think I'm involved in some grand conspiracy? That's absurd, Lisa."

"Is it really so absurd?" Lisa countered, her voice shaking with emotion. "Why else would you be so dismissive of everything I've found? You've seen the same things I have. Yet you refuse to acknowledge any of it. Why, George? What are you hiding?"

George sighed deeply, running a hand through his hair. "Lisa, it's not that simple. Yes, I've noticed things, but jumping to conclusions without solid proof can be dangerous. You're talking about people's lives and reputations. If we're wrong, we could ruin everything."

"And if we're right, we could save lives,"Lisa shot back. "We can't ignore this just because it's risky. We have to do something."

George's expression softened slightly, a hint of sympathy in his eyes. "I understand where you're coming from, but I can't jeopardize my position and my principles without more concrete evidence. You need to give me something more than just suspicions."

Lisa's shoulders slumped, feeling a mix of despair and determination. She took a deep breath, trying to convey the urgency and gravity of her findings.

"Listen to me carefully," Lisa began, her voice steady and resolute. "When I visited Sam's birthplace, I noticed that it's an extremely remote village. It's not the kind of place you'd expect someone like Mr. Ramson to settle in. He seemed to appear out of nowhere one day. Nobody knows where he came from, and the villagers couldn't provide any background about his past."

George raised an eyebrow, curiosity piqued. "What do you mean by that?"

"With his knowledge and wisdom, Ramson quickly became a key figure in the local community," Lisa continued. "He wasn't just a resident; he was someone the villagers looked up to, almost revered. His philanthropic approach, his way of helping people with their problems, and his deep understanding of various subjects endeared him to everyone. It wasn't long before his status in the village was elevated significantly."

George leaned in, listening intently. "That does sound unusual. But what exactly did you find so peculiar?"

Lisa took a deep breath, her eyes narrowing as she recalled the details. "His mannerisms and the items he used were unlike anything I've seen before. He had a habit of murmuring to himself in a language that no one could recognize. I tried recording it, but it was too faint and rapid to decipher."

George frowned, processing the

information. "That's definitely strange."

"Yes... I recall noticing that habit in Sam as well," George interjected, his brow furrowing in thought. "He would often murmur to himself during intense moments. It seemed odd at the time, but I never gave it much thought."

"Now it's all starting to make sense," Lisa continued, her voice gaining strength as she pieced together the puzzle. "And there's something else—something even more peculiar. Do you remember that time when Sam had that accident at our college, the one where he fell and injured himself?"

George nodded slowly, the memory coming back to him. "Yeah, I remember. He was pretty shaken up, but what about it?"

"I saw something unusual then," Lisa said, leaning in closer. "When Sam fell, I caught a glimpse of a golden tooth in his mouth. At first, I thought it was just an odddental choice. But then, recently, when Ramson slipped into the pool and I helped pullhim out, I saw the same thing—a golden tooth in his mouth too. It wasn't just a coincidence."

George's eyes widened in realization. "You're saying that the golden teeth aren't just for show?"

"Exactly," Lisa affirmed, her voice steady with conviction. "I believe those golden teeth are some sort of transmitters or communication devices. Think about it— Ramson and Sam both have them, and they both exhibit these strange, secretive behaviors. There's something they're hiding, something they're communicating that we can't hear."

George's face grew serious as he processed the implications. "This is bigger than I thought. If they're using these teeth to communicate, then there's a network, a system in place that's beyond what we've considered."

Lisa nodded, her thoughts swirling with possibilities. "And it explains why they're so meticulous about their projects and their isolation. They're not just avoiding anti- ecological endeavors out of principle— they're orchestrating something much larger, planning a significant initiative that we haven't fully grasped yet. Under the guise of philanthropy or corporate social responsibility, they could be aiming to secure something substantial," she speculated, her voice tinged with a mix of curiosity andconcern.

Taking a deep breath, Lisa continued, her voice steady with determination. "We need to uncover more about these transmitters and their purpose. Understanding the full extent of Ramson's influence on Sam and discerning their ultimate goal is crucial. And there's another layer to this— it's not just Ramson or Sam involved; there are others, and I have the list," she revealed, her tone carrying a sense of urgency and resolve as she prepared to delve deeper into the mystery.

George looked at her with a mix of apprehension and determination. "You're right. We need to get to the bottom of this. But we have to be careful, Lisa. If what you're saying is true, we could be stepping into something dangerous."

"Agreed," Lisa said, her eyes steely with resolve. "But we can't back down now. We have to see this through, no matter what it takes."

As Lisa continued her explanation, George's phone suddenly rang, its sharp tone cutting through the tension-filled air. The interruption was abrupt, jarring them out of their intense conversation. George glanced at the screen, his face paling as he recognized the caller.

"I'm sorry, Lisa. I need to take this... I'll be back in a moment," he said hurriedly, urgency evident in his voice.

Without waiting for her response, George stood up and walked briskly away, putting the phone to his ear. Lisa watched him go, her mind racing with the implications of their conversation and the sudden, unexplained call. She couldn't help but feel a surge of frustration and anxiety as she was left alone, her thoughts swirling with unanswered questions.

Standing there, she replayed their conversation in her mind, every detail and revelation mixing with her growing sense of unease. The idea that Sam and Ramson could be part of something far larger and more complex than she had initially imagined was both thrilling and terrifying.

Lisa took a deep breath, trying to calm herself. Glancing around at the bustling surroundings, she felt momentarily disoriented. The urgency of George's departure only added to her sense of impending danger and the need for answers.

As she waited for George to return, Lisa couldn't shake the feeling that time was running out. They were on the brink of uncovering something significant, but without George's cooperation and insights, she felt momentarily adrift. The minutes ticked by, and the sense of urgency grew with each passing second. But George didn't return.

Lisa's anxiety began to morph into a

gnawing fear. She tried calling his phone, but there was no answer. The restaurant around her buzzed with activity—the clinking of glasses and the murmur of conversations sharply contrasting with the storm of thoughts in her mind.

Feeling increasingly uneasy, Lisa decided she couldn't wait any longer. She left the table and walked out of the restaurant, scanning the street outside for any sign of George. The city lights glowed softly in the dusk, but George was nowhere to be seen.

* * * * *

"Lisa, can you spare sometime this evening?" George urged, his tone laced with urgency. "I've arranged a meeting with Professor Richard. He's an expert in this field, and his insights could really shed light on our concerns. This could be the breakthrough we need."

Lisa hesitated, her mind still reeling from the events of the previous day. "George, I'm still a bit bothered by what happened yesterday," she admitted, uncertainty in her voice. "Can we talk about it later? I need some time to process everything."

"I understand, Lisa," George said, softening his tone. "What happened yesterday was intense, and I don't want to rush you. But this meeting could be crucial. Professor Richard's knowledge and experience might be exactly what we need to piece together the puzzle. We need all hands-on deck for this. Please, just consider it."

Lisa took a deep breath, pondering his words. She knew he was right, though fear and anxiety still lingered. "Alright, George," she finally said, her voice steadying. "I'll be there. But you owe me an explanation— everything, from start to finish."

George nodded, visibly relieved. "Absolutely, Lisa. We'll go over everything thoroughly. It's crucial for our investigation," he affirmed, his voice carrying determination as they prepared to delve deeper into the matter.

As they finalized the details, Lisa couldn't shake the feeling that they were on the brink of something monumental. The sense of urgency mixed with a flicker of hope propelled her forward despite the lingering unease.

* * * * *

"Good evening, Professor," Lisa greeted warmly after George's introduction, extending her hand.

"Welcome, Lisa. George has given me a brief overview of your investigation," Professor Richard replied, shaking her hand and nodding in acknowledgment.

Despite feeling uneasy about someone else briefing the professor on her investigation, Lisa quietly accepted the chair offered to her. Her expression remained composed yet slightly tense, reflecting her internal conflict between maintaining control over her findings and recognizing the need for collaboration. She listened intently, prepared to contribute her insights and ensure the integrity of her research was respected.

"Yes, sir. My research has uncovered some intriguing mysteries that seem to defy conventional explanations," Lisa stated, her voice steady despite the gravity of her inquiry. "Before drawing any conclusions, I wanted to explore the possibility of alien involvement on Earth. I hope you don't thinkI'm being irrational."

"I completely understand, Lisa," the Professor reassured her, his tone calm and measured. "Your investigative work has beenquite impressive and thorough. Allow me to delve into the historical context, which might provide some clarity on the matters you're investigating."

Lisa nodded, grateful for the Professor's open-mindedness. "Thank you, Professor. I've been studying a series of patterns and anomalies among some successful young CEOs, including Sam and his father. Their backgrounds, behaviors, and certain peculiar traits, like their gold teeth,all seem to suggest something out of the ordinary. My observations extend only to one or two generations; beyond that, I'm unsure," she explained, her tone thoughtful yet uncertain as she considered the implications of her research.

The Professor leaned back in his chair, considering her words. "Your observations are indeed fascinating, Lisa," he said, a thoughtful expression on his face.

"It could be an alien invasion for a purpose," the Professor remarked, his tone contemplative.

"How can we jump to such a conclusion straight away?" George questioned skeptically. "All these intelligent people could be from a race or community on Earth, planning for something either positive or negative."

"It's a possibility! However, the evidence suggests that this is something beyond Earth. They could have a backend support on Earth as well. We cannot rule it out," the Professor explained steadily, his gaze shifting between Lisa and George.

"In various cultural texts and

records, we find mentions of alien encounters, both benevolent and malevolent," the Professor explained, gesturing towards the screen where he displayed images of ancient sculptures and paintings depicting UFOs. "These accounts span across civilizations and time periods, from the Sumerians to the Egyptians, and even in medieval manuscripts. They suggest that humanity has been interacting with extraterrestrial beings for thousands of years."

Lisa leaned forward, her curiosity piqued. "So many incidents of UFO sightings have been recorded. But are all these Unidentified Flying Objects truly of extraterrestrial origin?" she questioned.

The Professor nodded thoughtfully. "It's difficult to say definitively," he responded, his tone measured. "While some sightings may indeed be the result of rumours, misidentifications, or human-made objects used for military or scientific experiments, there is also a body of compelling evidence suggesting genuine extraterrestrial activity. For instance, the 1947 Roswell incident remains one of the most debated UFO events, with many convinced that the government recovered alien technology."

He clicked through more images, showing documents and declassified files. "In addition to sightings, there are numerous reports from credible sources, including military personnel and pilots, who have encountered flying objects that exhibit capabilities far beyond our current technological understanding—such as rapid acceleration, sudden changes in direction, and invisibility to radar."

Lisa's eyes widened as she absorbed the information. "So, do you believe that these advanced beings have been influencing human history and development?"

"Potentially, yes," the Professor agreed. "There are theories that suggest different alien factions might have had various motives—some benevolent, seeking to guide and aid humanity, and others malevolent, possibly seeking to exploit or control. The historical accounts of conflicts between these factions might have had profound impacts on human civilizations."

"Many governments are hesitant to disclose such information due to various security concerns," the Professor explained, his tone measured. "Throughout history, there have been instances where governments have suppressed or classified information related to UFO sightings and extraterrestrial encounters. This reluctance stems from a combination of factors, including concerns about national security, the potential impact on public morale, and the fear of societal upheaval."

Lisa nodded, absorbing the implications of the Professor's words. "So, despite the abundance of sightings and evidence, official confirmation has been elusive due to these factors?"

"Exactly," the Professor confirmed, adjusting his glasses. "However, there have been reports of research centers, labs, and covert operations dedicated to studying aliens and their technologies. These efforts are often shrouded in secrecy, with limited public awareness and oversight. It's a complex landscape where truth and speculation intertwine, making it challenging to separate fact from fiction."

"So, it's possible that alien groups have shared their knowledge with us, perhaps with the intention of advancing our civilization," George remarked thoughtfully, his eyes scanning the titles of the ancient texts.

"Indeed," the Professor affirmed, nodding in agreement. "Throughout history, there have been instances where human progress seems to have been accelerated by the introduction of unfamiliar technologies and concepts. These advancements often coincide with periods of significant cultural and technological leaps, suggesting external influences at play."

"In ancient texts, there are numerous references to advanced knowledge in areas such as mathematics, town planning, astronomy, medicine, agriculture, metallurgy, alchemy, scientific talents, spiritual practices, military strategies, mystical sciences, anti- gravity principles, and more, which could potentially be attributed to knowledge transferred by extraterrestrial beings," the Professor continued, his voice filled with scholarly enthusiasm.

"Books on ancient aeronautics, flight manuals found in the Indian subcontinent, and the construction of pyramid-like structures that seem beyond human capability, along with references to gods descending from the heavens and descriptions of advanced weaponry in religious texts—all of these lend credence to the possibility of ancient encounters with beings from beyond Earth," he explained passionately, emphasizing the global and longstanding nature of these accounts.

"The knowledge of astronomy found across different civilizations further substantiates the idea of extraterrestrial influence, as these societies demonstrated an understanding of celestial mechanics and astronomical phenomena that surpassed their technological capabilities," the Professor elaborated, his eyes alight with the excitement of unravelling ancient mysteries.

He gestured towards the reference books displayed on the table, inviting Lisa andGeorge to explore further.

"Their descent from space in spaceshipshas been visualized akin to gods arriving on Earth in chariots. The architecture of worship places also mirrors the shapes of space ships, particularly noticeable in the Indian subcontinent," the Professor remarked, his voice carrying a blend of scholarly interest and historical insight.

Lisa leaned in, her interest piqued by the implications of these revelations. "So, you're suggesting that aliens may have played a significant role in shaping human civilization?"

George interjected with a pertinent question, his brow furrowed in contemplation. "But why would such advanced beings come to Earth? What could their motivations havebeen?"

The Professor paused, considering George's inquiry before responding. "There are theories suggesting that Earth was used as a biosphere for alien experiments, though whether these experiments were benevolent or malevolent remains unknown," he explained, his voice carrying the weight of centuries of speculation and mystery.

"Some scriptures even propose that the human race is a hybrid creation of aliens and apes, designed to serve as workers to extract Earth's resources," the Professor added, his words sparking a flurry of questions in George's mind.

"What could these treasures be?" George inquired eagerly, leaning forward in anticipation of the answer.

"Diamonds, gold, and other precious metals and stones, perhaps even radioactive materials," the Professor replied, his tone measured and authoritative. "Throughout history, there have been records of frequent visits by aliens to Earth, evidenced by scriptures, paintings, and carvings."

As the conversation delved deeper into the mysteries of alien encounters and their potential impact on human history, Lisa couldn't help but interject with a pressing question. "Why would they do that?"

"To ensure that advanced civilizations persist, even in the face of potential extinction events," the Professor explained, his words carrying a sense of both wonder and foreboding.

"What are the possibilities?" George asked eagerly, his curiosity piqued by the implications of their discussion.

But Lisa, sensing the urgency of their situation, interrupted the discussion, her voice tinged with urgency. "Professor, what should I do? If I fail to present my case convincingly, I could become a target, and any further clues may be lost. Please advise," she implored, her eyes searching the Professor's for guidance.

The Professor nodded solemnly, acknowledging the gravity of Lisa's predicament. "You're absolutely right, Lisa," he agreed. "It's premature to present your case without strong evidence. Furthermore, considering that the majority of Fortune 500 companies seem to be led by these individuals, it's possible they hold positions in defense and government sectors as well. You'll need to gather more evidence to establish the facts."

"George, please support me until we reach a logical conclusion," Lisa implored as they left the meeting, her determination shining through despite the uncertainty of their path forward.

"Of course, Lisa. I'll do my best," George assured her, his commitment unwavering as they prepared to face the challenges ahead.

As they exited the meeting, Lisa couldn't shake the weight of the Professor's words. The enormity of their task loomed large, and she knew that every decision they made could have far-reaching consequences.

12

"Hi George! Have you reached Washington? How is Sam?" Lisa enquired eagerly.

"Yes, we're here. Tomorrow morning, let's meet at the Fortune CEO Initiative forum meeting," George confirmed.

The Fortune CEO Initiative is a forum for global corporate leaders committed to addressing the importance of Corporate Social Responsibility in saving the earth's ecology in Washington DC. To cover the event, Lisa and her team arrived at the location.

Meanwhile, George accompanied Sam for the meeting in Washington DC.

All attendees were staying in the same hotel for a couple of days, allowing for further discussions and networking outside of the formal meeting. The event saw the passing of numerous resolutions focusing on the contributions of corporate companies to environmental conservation. Key areas of focus included the production of environmentally friendly equipment, the conversion of sea water into drinking water, effective management of plastics, eco- friendly pesticides, and the promotion of non-conventional energy sources.

During the meeting, Sam's impassioned speech resonated deeply with the audience. "Dear friends," he began, his voice filled with emotion. "This is an unparalleled opportunity to serve humanity. It's a moment we've long awaited, and if we falter now, we risk losing everything. We must acknowledge our past mistakes and move forward with humility and determination. Let us embrace progress and commit to actions that promote peace and purity on our planet. Together, we can make a difference." With those words, Sam concluded his opening remarks, leaving a profound impact on all those present.

In the evening, Lisa reached out to Samson, inviting him to join her for dinner. "Sorry Lisa," Sam replied regretfully. "I have an important meeting tonight. I won't be ableto make it."

Undeterred, Lisa then contacted George. "Hey George, would you like to grab dinner together tonight?" she asked, hopefulfor his company.

"Sure, what time and where?" George responded, eager to catch up. "Let's ask Samto join us."

Lisa hesitated for a moment before replying, "Actually, it seems Sam already hasplans for a meeting tonight."

Curious about this unexpected meeting,George decided to investigate. "What meeting?" he asked Sam when he called him."Did Lisa contact you?"

With a knowing smile, Sam replied, "You should go ahead and join her. I'll manage." And with that, he left the call, leaving George puzzled yet intrigued by the mystery surrounding Sam's sudden meeting.

George noticed that the call was not disconnected. As George listened in stunned silence, he couldn't believe what he was hearing. Ramson was involved in the conversation, which was highly unusual for a meeting of CEOs.

Ramson's voice confirmed George's suspicions. "It is overdue now. We have to implement our plan as quickly as possible," Ramson stated urgently.

Realization dawned on George as he processed Ramson's words. The mention of Lisa, the reporter, and her discoveries about the transmitter in their teeth sent a chill down his spine. It was clear that Sam and Ramson were discussing something far moresinister than corporate matters.

Feeling a sense of urgency, George remained silent, keeping the call muted as he listened intently to the unfolding conversation. It was becoming increasingly evident that there was more to Sam and Ramson than met the eye, and George knew he had stumbled upon something grave.

The call abruptly disconnected, George found himself unable to listen any further. Hastily, he relayed the startling revelation to Lisa.

"Lisa! You are right," George exclaimed,his voice tinged with urgency.

Understanding the gravity of the situation, Lisa nodded solemnly. "Let's work together and delve into this. We need to present our findings at the right forum, but until then, confidentiality is crucial to avoid any complications," she emphasized, her voice steady with determination.

With a determined expression, Georgereplied, "I agree."

Their conversation marked the beginning of a collaborative effort to uncover the truth behind Sam and Ramson's mysterious agenda, one that would require careful investigation and discretion.

* * * * *

13

The recent lunar missions by India's Chandrayan and China's Chang'e have yielded ground-breaking discoveries, igniting global interest and concern. Chandrayan's landing on the dark side of the moon revealed the presence of a substantial spaceship on its far side, while Chang'e's subsequent mission provided corroborating evidence of similar findings. Additionally, images captured by the lunar rover indicated unusual movements within the moon's expansive craters, raising questions about the nature and origin of thesephenomena.

In response to these significant developments, the General Assembly invoked Resolution 377A(V), known as "Uniting for Peace," which was adopted on 3 November 1950. This resolution empowers the Assembly to convene an "emergency special session" within 24 hours in the event of threats to international peace and security, particularly in cases where the Security

Council fails to reach a consensus.

The invocation of Resolution 377A(V) underscores the urgency and gravity of the situation surrounding the lunar discoveries. With the potential implications for global stability and security, the international community is poised to convene an emergency session to deliberate on the implications of these findings and formulate a collective response.

As nations prepare to gather for the emergency session, there is a palpable sense of anticipation and apprehension regarding the next steps. The Assembly's deliberations will likely focus on assessing the significance of the lunar discoveries, evaluating potential risks, and charting a course of action to address any threats posed by these unprecedented developments.

In the face of uncertainty and speculation, the international community stands ready to uphold the principles of peace, cooperation, and collective security enshrined in Resolution 377A(V). The emergency session represents a crucial opportunity for dialogue, collaboration, and decisive action to safeguard the interests of all nations in the face of emerging challenges from beyond the Earth's atmosphere.

"Good. Then convene the meeting immediately in coordination with the Security Council," the Secretary General ordered, prompting a high-level debate to commence.

"It is evident that the spaceship doesn't belong to any country on Earth," one official asserted.

"Yes, there is evidence of Alien ships visiting the Earth for a long time," another added.

"True. Ancient civilizations have recorded the visits of Aliens in their epics, literary works, and inscriptions," a third member chimed in.

"We are all aware of Alien footprints at Egyptian Pyramids, in the history books of Greeks, Sumerian inscriptions, Literature of India and Tibet, and many more," others acknowledged.

Various members expressed their views, acknowledging the historical evidence of Alien visitations across different cultures and civilizations.

"So many member nations had doubts about research works carried out by various nations confidentially, and there were numerous rumors about identified areas for that," one member nation commented, highlighting concerns about the secrecy surrounding research efforts.

"In this crisis moment, what should we do? We need not dwell on the past; the present is in front of us. Let's focus on finding a solution," the Secretary General advised, urging forward-thinking approaches.

"It is very clear that the Alien race is much more advanced than us, and it will be very difficult to face them. We don't have any clue about their future course of action or their capabilities. Therefore, it's best for the First Committee on Disarmament and International Security to handle this and suggest remedial action," another member proposed.

The committee considers all disarmament and international security matters within the scope of the Charter, or relating to the powers and functions of any other organ of the United Nations. It promotes general principles of cooperation in the maintenance of international peace and security, as well as principles governing disarmament and the regulation of armaments. Additionally, it supports cooperative arrangements and measures aimed at strengthening stability through lower levels of armaments.

"Let us have some evidence and related facts. Alien movement on the moon need not be merely an exploration; it could be much more. It is definitely connected with Earth. It may be preparatory work to encroach upon humanity. Until we have more clues, let us remain cautious and active," the meeting concluded after forming a Special Committee to probe further.

14

"Why are you so suspicious, and when did it begin?" one of the UN committee members asked Lisa.

Lisa's request had been taken into consideration, given the gravity of the investigation and the situation at hand.

"When I met Sam, I couldn't help but notice his exceptional strength. He rarely sleeps, from what I've observed. His memory and energy are extraordinary. Moreover, he seems deeply committed to nature and its preservation," Lisa explained, pausing briefly before continuing.

"When Sam got injured, he wasn't allowed to consult a dentist, despite bleeding. I noticed his back teeth appeared to be made of gold. Later, during interviews with individuals purported to be part of the alienrace, I observed similar gold teeth. It dawned on me that these teeth were actually microphone-speakers. These individuals seemed to murmur amongst themselves, which I now understand as communication.

"During a visit to Samson's residence, I witnessed an incident where his father, Ramson, fell into a pool. While pulling him out with Sam's help, I noticed he also had a similar gold tooth mic," Lisa explained, her voice tinged with a mix of concern and intrigue. "Sam hasn't allowed me further access to investigate, which has prevented me from drawing any conclusions. At the time, I assumed he was reciting some sort of chant, but only recently have I started connecting these observations," she continued, her thoughts reflecting a growing realization that there might be more to these incidents than meets the eye.

"Was there any other evidence to support your suspicions?" someone asked.

"Yes, indeed," Lisa replied. "The most striking revelation came when I saved Ramson. I noticed that he didn't have belly button as humans do. Now, how could a person born on Earth lack such belly button? I consulted medical experts, who informed me that while it's rare, some individuals are born with unusual belly button due to surgical history. However, I kept this observation to myself. Now, I believe they are not born, but rather created prototypes or hybrid bodies that have infiltrated our society."

"That's quite remarkable, Lisa," a committee member remarked, impressed by her diligence in uncovering these individuals.

"The credit truly goes to my boss. He suggested I make a film about the most successful young CEOs, and that's where it all began," Lisa explained. "Starting with Samson, I delved into their backgrounds and soon realized something was amiss. Upon tracing their family histories, I found no traces of their forefathers. These individuals gradually integrated into rural communities, establishing identities before advancing to urban areas and positioning their next generations into key roles. Initially, nobody believed me," Lisa remarked.

"Can you conclude in toto," the

Chairman asked.

"Yes, Sir. They belong to an intelligent race from outer space and have taken up prominent positions worldwide, exerting influence over corporate and government decisions. Their presence in fields such as nuclear energy, defense, and government is largely unknown. Our findings are just the beginning," Lisa concluded.

"It is true. The exact number of aliens on Earth is an unknown fact. If we react adversely, it may boomerang to us. I should not say, even in this meeting also, some may be there," the Chairman remarked with a frightening smile.

"The only solution is to call for a meeting of identified Alien families and to find out the reason for their intrusion and to vacate the Earth's and the moon's surface," one member suggested.

"Perfect. Please consolidate the details provided by Lisa and her team, along with information from other sources, and prepare a presentation for a meeting three days from now. Ensure the presence of listed alien groups also," the Chairman concluded.

* * * * *

15

The emergency meeting of the United Nations commenced.

Identified families of the Alien race, including Samson and Ramson, were present.

There was a pin-drop silence as the meeting began. To kick-start the proceedings, there was a moment of hesitation.

Finally, the Secretary General of the United Nations initiated, his voice carrying a mix of gravity and curiosity, "We understand from the recent incidents in and around Earth that our planet is facing significant challenges. Based on the evidence presented, there are implications that suggest you may be involved as troublemakers and intruders. What do you say? Where are you from?"

"Our parents are from the Andromeda galaxy," Samson revealed straightforwardly, his voice steady and unflinching, leaving everyone in the room stunned into silence.

"How can you enter the Earth without our permission?" one member asked, voicing the incredulity felt by many.

"And with whose permission are you conducting launches to the Moon or Mars?" countered one of the Alien group members.

"We are sure that there is nobody on those planets, and we are conducting tests and exploration, unlike you," another member retorted, their tone tinged with anger.

"You have knowingly intruded where there is an existing race, and it is wrong to enter and seize their opportunities," anothermember criticized.

Then Samson shouted, "We are not intruders," clearly displeased with their lineof questioning.

One leader pointed out, "If not, who areyou? How many of you are here? What is yourmotto? You have captured the entire world for what reason? So many youth on

Earth are left jobless due to your invasion. If you were not here, our younger generation could be managing. It is purely because of you. You should be ashamed of this."

Ramson stepped forward, assuming a dignified posture as he prepared to plead on behalf of the alien group. His demeanor was calm yet commanding, embodying a sense of authority that demanded attention in the room.

Suddenly, the Chairman received alarming news and announced, "Some spaceships are converging over all the major cities and capitals of various countries. The situation is dire, and people are terrified."

In response, one of the members shouted at the alien group, his voice filled with anger and accusation. "Now you've shown your true colors! This cannot go unpunished. You will face the consequences," he declared vehemently, his words echoing through the room.

Without further deliberation, all

Aliensare arrested on the spot as per the given directives.

Their explanations are not considered, and they are not allowed to complete their pleading.

* * * * *

16

A world army was swiftly formed, and a Committee comprising Defense Ministers and Army Commanders of the Security Council was given the authority to handle the situation.

A decision was made to repel the alien ships, as they posed a potential threat to the capital cities, leaders, and the public. Fighter jets were deployed to intercept the alien ships at major locations.

Fighter jets across all capital cities were swiftly grouped and deployed, their engines roaring to life as they prepared for action. Orders were issued urgently to intercept and drive away the alien ships that had caused a ripple of alarm and uncertainty across the globe. The skies buzzed with activity as military commanders coordinated efforts to safeguard their respective territories, while tensions mounted both on the ground and in the air. The world held its breath, uncertain of what the next moments would bring in this unprecedented encounter between Earth and the Andromeda.

However, despite the efforts of the fighter jets, the alien ships continued to advance toward the major cities at a steadypace.

Command control continued to issue instructions to the fighter jets, but despite their efforts, they were unable to halt the advance of the alien spaceships toward the densely populated areas of cities.

With no response from inside the alien ships, it was decided that there was no alternative but to attack them, as world leaders feared the devastating consequences if the alien ships were allowed to cover the major cities and cause harm.

The world army launched an assault on the alien ships, but their efforts proved futileas the alien ships seemed impervious to the attacks.

An emergency online meeting was convened with the Presidents and Prime Ministers of Member countries of the

United Nations to address the pressing issue at hand.

"Dear friends, today we are faced with a dire situation. In order to preserve mankind, we find ourselves with no other recourse than a nuclear attack. However, we must acknowledge the uncertainty of its effectiveness. There is a possibility that such action could have detrimental consequences for us, especially considering that the alien spaceships have already encroached upon various cities across the globe," remarked theSecretary General.

"Why can't we wait until they take the first step? By initiating an attack, we may beprovoking them unnecessarily. If they retaliate, what position will we be left in? Perhaps we should attempt negotiation," one member advised cautiously.

"You may have a valid point. However, consider this: if all the space ships simultaneously launch attacks on major cities, the loss of life could be catastrophic, potentially wiping out a significant portion of mankind within a single day. It's a grim scenario, which is why we feel compelled to take action to prevent such a possibility. Nevertheless, we must seek the advice of experts before proceeding," the Secretary General explained, emphasizing the urgency of the situation.

"We can do one thing. We can launch a nuclear attack on the mother ship on Moon,"one member advised urgently.

"Do you think we have that much time?" The Director General chuckled nervously,even in such a serious situation.

Suddenly, the network was intercepted,and the screen flickered to life with the image of the Commander of the aliens. The members of the august forum were visibly shaken.

"I request that you lower your weapons and refrain from provoking us before we can discuss anything further," the Commander of the aliens advised calmly but firmly, his presence commanding respect despite the tense stand off.

"What the hell is going on? How can you intrude like this? The human race has existed after millions of years of struggle. How can you simply dominate us all of a sudden?" One member questioned emotionally, reflecting the shock and anger of the assembly.

The hall vibrated with the booming laughter of the Commander of the Aliens.

"Don't say all these things. 'Survival of the fittest' is your theory. Humans have just 0.01% of all life, but have destroyed more than 80% of wild mammals. 75% of the Earth's ice-free land has been significantly altered by human activity. 90% of global wetlands have been lost within 300 years of your hopeless science. Water polluted by you is killing both humans and marine life," the Alien Commander paused, emphasizing the impact of human activity on the planet.

"Don't talk about your innocence. Wherever you are strong, you dominate, and wherever you are weak, you surrender. Here you are weak, and hence surrender," the Commander of Aliens concluded with a confident tone.

"What is the purpose of this intrusion? We are living peacefully on the planet. It seems that you are from an advanced race. Why you want to capture us ? Either please help us in advancement or leave us for our destiny. We will reach your stage one day", one senior member requested.

"There is no equivalence between your capabilities and ours. We intend to establish ourselves on this planet, which is imperative," declared the Alien Commander with unwavering resolve. "I cannot elaborate further. Whether you surrender or resist, we will capture you. This is our final decision," he asserted firmly, his words echoing through the tense atmosphere of the forum.

"Dear friend, please note that so many residents of your planet were arrested and they are in our custody. Don't forget this fact," the Secretary General cautioned the Commander of Aliens.

"Ridiculous!" the Commander of Aliens shouted. "Nobody from us is on Earth. You are confused and confusing."

"It is true. If you want you can talk to them now. Please wait for some time", the Secretary General of the UN advised.

After some time, some of the CEOs and the members of their families were brought to the meeting for the interaction with the Alien Commander.

"Dear friend, these are all have occupied key positions and proved to be culprits and arrested by us. They are about to be prosecuted. If you leave us peacefully, we can hand them over to you. What do you say?" One member of the forum offered.

"Who are these creatures? We don't know them. You do whatever you want. Be prepared for consequences. I've lost my patience," the Commander of the Aliens shouted, his voice resonating with frustrationand urgency.

"Wait, Joe. Why are you so aggressive? I've never seen you so emotional before," Ramson interjected calmly, attempting to diffuse the escalating tension.

There was pin-drop silence. Everyone was confused and unable to grasp what was happening.

"How do you know me? Who are you?" Joe, the Commander of the Aliens, asked in astonishment.

"After a long time, Joe, this is Lee," Ramson, also known as Lee, replied calmly.

All the spectators were in a state of confusion, trying to understand the conversation.

"Mr. President, you're here! I can't believe this," Joe exclaimed, his voice filled with astonishment and a touch of disbelief.

"Yes, we are here," Lee paused for a moment before continuing. "Why are you causing suffering to the people of this planet?" he questioned.

"I am sorry, President. We were not aware of your presence here. We haven't attacked anyone. But these people got confused and provoked us, so we took this stand," Joe replied politely.

"These people don't know your intentions. They only see your actions, hence the confusion. Now that you've clarified, please vacate," Lee requested expressing a hope for safe departure and future understanding. "I hope you'll fare well."

"Thank you, President. Goodbye. Good luck to all of you and to the human race of Earth. We may return one day, with advance

notice," Joe said with a smile before disconnecting.

All the members became silent spectators to the lengthy conversation, slowlyregaining consciousness.

"If you permit me, I'd like to address you," Lee requested the Secretary General.

* * * * *

17

"Dear fellow humans,

This is Lee, President of the Planet of Andromeda Galaxy.

Let me clarify one thing. Until now, you were fighting with the members of our neighboring planet of the same Galaxy. Now they have returned. No worries about them. They obey me.

"We were once like you, millions of years ago. Through countless technological advancement, we inadvertently harmed our own ecosystem and engaged in conflicts among ourselves. It was only after enduring immense devastation that we realized the crucial importance of nature, peace, and the sanctity of life. Learning from our mistakes, we began to live harmoniously with nature, utilizing its resources responsibly for our well-being without causing harm," Joe explained, his voice carrying a sombre reflection on his species' journey of growth and enlightenment.

We were the frequent visitors to your planet. Earlier, we have visited and shared our knowledge on so many occasions. After many ups and downs, the human race on planet Earth started in a different direction once again and explored new things. We are keenly watching you. You have noticed so many UFOs in and around you. But we have advanced technology. We can attain maximum speed, and our Spaceships have many features like disappearing and managing Radars. Knowingly, we are hiding ourselves, as you may not use the knowledge transferred for securing your planet and may try to use it for selfish things, especially for destruction. In reality, we are eager to share our knowledge with the right people at the right time.

We have set up our space stations and other establishments on the surface of the moon, specifically in the caves of the dark side, to avoid visibility.

Unfortunately, after many eras of peace, we encountered some trouble and were required to vacate our planet. Ramson's revelation brought a moment of reflection.

The forum listened in complete silence,each member captivated yet unsure whether they were witnessing reality or merely caught in a dream like state.

Suddenly, we had to evacuate. All species had to be shifted, presenting us withnumerous challenges.

A neutron star approached us, signaling the urgency of our evacuation. This wasn't just a problem for us; it affected four more planets. You have witnessed the situation of our neighboring planet.

The impending threat of the neutron star with its extreme surface temperature of around 550,000 K gave us approximately 100 years to prepare. However, the constant meteor storms, calamitous shifts in seasons, bursts of radiation, and the deformation of our planet's core and crust by the neutron star's tidal forces posed significant risks to life on our planet. The gravity from the neutron star would eventually tear away our planet's surface, leading to its destruction.

Given these dire circumstances, families faced the potential of being broken up if we delayed preparations until the last minute. Therefore, it was decided to relocate to a suitable planet that could replicate our technology, infrastructure, and ecosystem. We chose Planet Y near Barnard's Star, a red dwarf located about six light-years from Earth in the constellation of Ophiuchus. Despite its proximity, Barnard's Star has a dim apparent magnitude and is invisible to the unaided eye. Our knowledge of this star dates back 130 years, to when we first began efforts to establish ourselves on Planet Y.

"Initially, we created the ecological system and subsequently streamlined it according to our needs. Our people were divided into three groups: scientists and professionals were stationed at Planet Y, continuously building infrastructure and meeting other requirements. Additionally, some were placed on the Moon and Europa to support those on Earth. Moon workstations were dedicated solely to supporting our operations on Earth, while the Europa space station coordinated between us and Planets X and Y. Wise men, leaders, and other important individuals were temporarily relocated to Earth. We systematically shifted our people onto Earth," Ramson paused as someone raised an objection.

"You must have consulted us and obtained permission. How can you expect post facto approvals like this?" someone questioned.

"True. But it doesn't work. Just now we have seen the live example. You won't believe us. Moreover, we have two motives for doingso.

The first one is not known to you. Thousands of years back, we supported the human race in developing their scientific approach. We conducted numerous excavations on Earth. When you were at the beginning, we tried to inculcate the scientific approach in you. We taught Astronomy, Alchemy, Mathematics, and many other basics. We established contacts with specific civilizations to expedite development on Earth."

"But... unfortunately, when you gained momentum, you focused on physical comforts,which really spoiled the ecological system and made life miserable for future generations,"Ramson continued.

"Then it was decided to mingle with you for a generation as a stopgap arrangement and subsequently shift permanently to Planet Y. For that, I personally led the team. We all came with a motto to infiltrate your corporate world and influence developments, projects, and modern science with a touch of humanity and responsibility, which is lacking now."

"Accordingly, we created hybrid bodies with local features of various countries and systematically entered into hamlets of the world first. Once identity was established, we shifted to urban areas and used our next generation to work on proposed projects. Our second generation occupied key positions with a positive motto of correcting you. You may like it or not, but it is true. We wanted to go back silently, passing a message. However, the truth cannot hide. It was revealed," Ramson explained.

"We planned the rehabilitation process for around 50 years, out of which 30 years were to be spent on Earth and the rest of the period on the Moon. There were four planets nearby us that were also in trouble. We have an agreement of non-invasion into other territories."

"The recent space ships that entered your planet were from our neighboring planet. They were also in search of suitable locations, but unlike us, they came to negotiate with you for shelter. When they found out that we were already present here, they left. Our presence here must have helped in avoiding friction. Knowingly or unknowingly, our presence here saves you; otherwise, my fellow friends might have destroyed this planet due to a communication gap," Ramson explained.

"Anyway, now we are leaving your planet. We don't want to leave any room for friction. We will be departing from Earth after completing certain formalities on the Moon. It may take a little more time to evacuate the Moon. However, we have created a lot of infrastructure on the Moon, which will be handed over to you after due training. For this project, my son Sam will lead with his technological partners. They are all accustomed to Earth's local conditions, so they may please be allowed to continue here for coordination purposes. The rest of us will leave soon."

"During our stay, we realized that there was something to be done on Earth. You are also our fellow beings, and it is our responsibility to correct you," Ramson continued. "Through the Agricultural Revolution and Industrial Revolution, you have advanced, but not in the proper direction. While seeking shelter, it was planned to correct your path."

"We took a chance to seek shelter and guide you in the right direction. I am sorry to say this. The reason for our next generation not marrying here is to avoid friction and to ensure 100% evacuation."

"Anyway, now the secret is revealed. We want it to be peaceful and without any rupture. Unfortunately, some misunderstandings are there. We are happy that we are here at the right time to save you from our fellow planet's invasion."

"Now we understand that it is time to vacate. Thanks for everything. Goodbye."

* * * * *

18

The entire globe was thrown into shock as the news spread like wildfire. People everywhere began to suspect the intelligent individuals around them, prompting those perceived as exceptionally intelligent to dramatically prove their identities. Ramson'smessage to humanity went viral, dominating conversations in every nook and cranny. The topic was dissected and debated endlessly, with countless interpretations emerging fromall corners of the world.

On the other side, preparations for the return journey of the alien groups were in full swing. The handover and takeover activities reached their peak, creating a frenzy of final arrangements. Staff members of major companies, now aware that they had been working under alien leadership, were left in shock. The departure of their CEOs led to promotions for the next level of officials, sparking celebrations tempered with regret for the sudden loss of such influential and philanthropic leaders.

Samson was appointed as the project director for the mission of knowledge transfer and maintenance of alien technologies, offering a glimmer of hope to humanity.

On the day of departure, various spaceships of different sizes and shapes converged on the designated location, illuminating the night sky and turning it as bright as day with their luminous lights. The space vehicles, each uniquely shaped— vertical, cylindrical, saucer-like, and more— created a spectacular and awe-inspiring display, marking the culmination of an unprecedented chapter in human history.

All the identified families arrived at the location, burdened by their heavy memories. The atmosphere was filled with mixed emotions— heartache, grief, and deep sadness. Tears filled many eyes as the solemnity of the moment sank in.

Placards with the caption "Please

come back soon" were held up by the crowds gathered outside the barricades, their voices quivering with emotion as they expressed

their heartfelt farewells. The scene was a poignant mix of sorrow and hope, reflecting the profound impact of the impending departure on everyone present.

"I'm sorry for causing you trouble. I was too harsh," Lisa admitted, unable to meet Sam's gaze. Her eyes filled with tears, and she could say no more.

"Don't blame yourself. If our roles were reversed, I would have probably done the same," Sam reassured her, his expression sincere.

"I've been given permission to stay. I'll be back once I settle some issues on the moon. Now I can find a wife on Earth," Sam's voice trembled slightly.

"Really?" Lisa's eyes widened in surprise.

"Yes, it's true. I'm searching for the right match," Sam confirmed.

In a sudden, unexpected move, Lisa slapped him. The onlookers remained silent, watching the exchange.

The spaceships embarked on their new journey, carrying hope for all. As they took off, the sky was filled with the dazzling sight of numerous luminous vessels, resembling a multitude of hydrogen balloons with lights, akin to a grand festival of fireworks.

Everyone there felt a sudden vacuum and gloominess in their lives, an unspoken embarrassment settling over them. Slowly, the gatherings began to disperse. As they were leaving, George made a call, his voice firm, **"Now we can begin our operation."**

* * * * *